Luke silently vo̶ anything to help Abby keep custody of her kids.

Admiration for her fluttered through him, and he became aware of several things at once, like the fact that Abby's sweet scent filled the room and that she was clad in only a pale, frilly nightgown.

He had an overwhelming desire to learn every inch of her. His body reacted to his thoughts, filling with a tension that seemed unbearable.

But it was a tension he wouldn't, couldn't, follow through on.

And in that instant, he knew exactly what he wanted to do. It wouldn't solve the problem, but it just might give Abby a fighting chance.

"Abby." He stood and faced her. "Marry me."

Dear Reader,

Happy New Year! And happy reading, too—starting with the wonderful Ruth Langan and *Return of the Prodigal Son*, the latest in her newest miniseries, THE LASSITER LAW. When this burned-out ex-agent comes home looking for some R and R, what he finds instead is a beautiful widow with irresistible children and a heart ready for love. *His* love.

This is also the month when we set out on a twelve-book adventure called ROMANCING THE CROWN. Linda Turner starts things off with *The Man Who Would Be King*. Return with her to the island kingdom of Montebello, where lives—and hearts—are about to be changed forever.

The rest of the month is terrific, too. Kylie Brant's CHARMED AND DANGEROUS concludes with *Hard To Tame*, Carla Cassidy continues THE DELANEY HEIRS with *To Wed and Protect*, Debra Cowan offers a hero who knows the heroine is *Still the One,* and Monica McLean tells us *The Nanny's Secret*. And, of course, we'll be back next month with six more of the best and most exciting romances around.

Enjoy!

[signature]

Leslie J. Wainger
Executive Senior Editor

Please address questions and book requests to:
Silhouette Reader Service
U.S.: 3010 Walden Ave., P.O. Box 1325, Buffalo, NY 14269
Canadian: P.O. Box 609, Fort Erie, Ont. L2A 5X3

To Wed
and Protect

CARLA CASSIDY

Silhouette

INTIMATE MOMENTS™

Published by Silhouette Books

America's Publisher of Contemporary Romance

If you purchased this book without a cover you should be aware
that this book is stolen property. It was reported as "unsold and
destroyed" to the publisher, and neither the author nor the
publisher has received any payment for this "stripped book."

 SILHOUETTE BOOKS

ISBN 0-373-27196-4

TO WED AND PROTECT

Copyright © 2002 by Carla Bracale

All rights reserved. Except for use in any review, the reproduction
or utilization of this work in whole or in part in any form by any
electronic, mechanical or other means, now known or hereafter
invented, including xerography, photocopying and recording, or in
any information storage or retrieval system, is forbidden without
the written permission of the editorial office, Silhouette Books,
300 East 42nd Street, New York, NY 10017 U.S.A.

All characters in this book have no existence outside the imagination of
the author and have no relation whatsoever to anyone bearing the same
name or names. They are not even distantly inspired by any individual
known or unknown to the author, and all incidents are pure invention.

This edition published by arrangement with Harlequin Books S.A.

® and TM are trademarks of Harlequin Books S.A., used under license.
Trademarks indicated with ® are registered in the United States Patent
and Trademark Office, the Canadian Trade Marks Office and in other
countries.

Visit Silhouette at www.eHarlequin.com

Printed in U.S.A.

Books by Carla Cassidy

CARLA CASSIDY

has written over forty books for Silhouette. In 1995, she won Best Silhouette Romance, and in 1998, she won a Career Achievement Award for Best Innovative Series, both from *Romantic Times Magazine*.

Carla believes the only thing better than a good book to read is a good story to write. She's looking forward to writing many more and bringing hours of pleasure to readers.

Chapter 1

The place looked as if it had been abandoned for years, but Luke knew it had only stood empty for a little less than a year. However, before abandonment the house and surrounding acreage had been owned by a cantankerous, eccentric old man who, rumor had it, had believed himself from the planet Zutar and spent most of his time attempting to contact fellow space creatures.

But Zutarian Arthur Graham had died almost a year earlier, and as far as Luke Delaney knew, the ramshackle house had not been entered since.

The early morning sun beat relentlessly on Luke's head as he got out of his car and approached the front door. If not for the car sitting out front, Luke would have assumed the house was still vacant. There were certainly no signs of life and no indication that any work at all had been done to make the house look more inviting.

The wood on the house was weathered to a dull gray, and thick weeds choked the path that led to a dangerously sagging front porch.

Luke had received a call the day before from a Mrs. Abigail Graham, asking if he'd be interested in meeting her here first thing this morning to discuss some carpentry work she wanted done on the place.

He'd been surprised. First and foremost because he hadn't heard any rumors that anyone had moved into the old Graham place, and usually the minute a stranger appeared in or around town, the gossipmongers went into action.

Luke had instantly agreed to meet with her, intrigued to see the interior of the place. After all, it wasn't everyday you got to see the living environment of a space alien.

And he had to admit, he was equally intrigued to meet the woman who owned the smoky, deep voice that had called him the day before. That voice had instantly conjured up visions of a lush brunette or a sultry blonde and had reminded Luke that it had been far too long since he'd enjoyed the company of a pretty lady.

Of course, Abigail Graham was probably sixty years old and as crazy as her infamous relative, he thought as he stepped up on the front porch.

With his first step onto the wooden porch, it instantly became apparent how imminent repairs were needed. The wood was rotten, and a hole was just in front of the door, indicating that somebody'd had a foot go completely through the rotten wood.

He carefully maneuvered around the hole and knocked on the door. It was opened immediately. The woman who stood before him was certainly no sixty-year-old. With long dark hair cascading around her slim shoulders and framing her slender face, she was definitely on the right side of thirty.

"Abigail Graham?" Luke asked, noting that her eyes were the shade of spring...a soft, lovely green that shimmered like the sea in the bright sunshine.

However, one of those beautiful green eyes appeared slightly swollen, and a hint of a bruise peeked beneath makeup at the corner.

"Yes, and you must be Luke Delaney."

He backed up as she stepped out and across the hole. "I'm assuming this is what you called me about?" he asked, gesturing to the porch.

She nodded. "I knew it was rather unstable but didn't realize just how dangerous it was until my son's foot went through it yesterday."

That sexy voice of hers shot a new wave of pleasure through him. Looking at her certainly wasn't difficult, either. Mrs. Abigail Graham, he reminded himself. A married woman sporting the hint of a black eye—and certainly none of his business.

"Was he hurt?" Luke asked, eyeing the hole.

"Thankfully no. His tennis shoe got scuffed and it scared him, but he wasn't hurt." She smiled, and Luke felt the jolt of that gorgeous smile deep in the pit of him, like that lick of heat he got when he took a swallow of good Scotch.

"Why don't you come on inside and we can discuss the repair work," she suggested. She stepped over the hole to the front door.

He followed her into the house and tried not to notice how sexy her shapely bottom looked in her tight jeans. The living room, although starkly furnished, was spotlessly clean and decorated in desert shades.

From someplace else in the house he could hear the sound of a television playing what sounded like cartoons.

She gestured him to the sofa, and he sat. "The man at the lumberyard said you were the best carpenter in town," she explained. "He was the one who gave me your name and number."

She perched on the edge of a chair facing the sofa. "So, what will it take to repair the porch?"

"I can't repair it. It needs to come down altogether and a new one built."

A frown creased her forehead, and she caught her lower lip between her teeth. She had luscious full lips, and Luke wondered idly if they would be as soft and inviting as they looked.

"How much is all this going to cost?" she finally asked with a sigh.

Luke stood and pulled a measuring tape from his pocket. "Why don't we go out and get some measurements, then I can give you an estimate." He had a feeling he wasn't going to make much profit on this job.

It was obvious that money was an issue. Anyone who chose to live in this ramshackle place had to have made the decision because they couldn't afford anything better.

"Okay, I'll be right back." She got up, hurried down the hallway and disappeared into the first doorway on the right.

Luke once again looked around the room. On second glance, he saw the work that needed to be done. Windowsills needed to be refinished or painted. The hardwood floor was scuffed and worn. But those things were cosmetic. The rotten porch was something different. She was lucky nobody had been seriously hurt on it.

She returned from the bedroom and they gingerly stepped out on the rotten porch. "This is a bad accident waiting to happen," he said as they stepped off the porch. "If you have me build you a new one, would you want it to be the same size?"

He watched as she gazed at the porch thoughtfully. Lordy, but she was pretty. Her clear, creamy skin looked soft and touchable, and her dark hair was a perfect foil for her startling green eyes.

"It's a pretty good size, isn't it?" she said thoughtfully.

"Sure," he agreed. "It's big enough to hold a couple of chairs and a potted plant or two."

"Then let's keep the new one the same size."

He nodded. "Let's get the measurements."

As she took the end of the tape measure from him, he smelled her fragrance, a soft whisper of something sweetly feminine and clean. It was probably a good thing the woman was married. Otherwise she would be a huge temptation, and Luke was trying not to walk the path of temptation.

"How long have you been here?" he asked as he gestured for her to go to the opposite side of the porch.

"We arrived on Tuesday and have spent the last couple of days having trash hauled off. Apparently my uncle was a bit of a pack rat."

Luke made a mental note of the measurement, then motioned her to the side of the porch. "Arthur was your uncle? Nobody around here knew he had any relatives."

"Actually, he was a great-uncle, but I never met him in person."

"That's all I need," he said and hit the button on the tape measure to retract the tape. "He was a bit of a character, your great-uncle Arthur."

Her cheeks flushed prettily as she met him at the base of the steps leading to the porch. "Poor Uncle Arthur. My father used to say he was a bolt whose nut was screwed on crooked."

Luke laughed at the apt description of the old man. "He was certainly colorful," he agreed. "He sometimes showed up in town with aluminum foil antennas wrapped around his head, said he was picking up signals from space."

She winced, then gave another one of her pretty smiles. "Well, I hate to disappoint the town gossips, but I don't intend to take up where Uncle Arthur left off," she replied.

Luke grinned. "Don't worry, we've got plenty of other odd people here in Inferno to keep the gossips busy.'' He hated to think how often in the past he had kept the gossip mill busy.

''Where are you from?'' he asked curiously.

''Uh…back east.''

He grinned. ''Back east as in New York or back east as in East India?''

''Uh…Chicago. We're from Chicago.''

Luke didn't know exactly how he knew, but he was fairly certain she was lying. Her gaze didn't quite meet his, and there was a hint of unnatural color to her cheeks that let him know she wasn't being truthful. Again he reminded himself that the lovely lady was none of his business.

At that moment the front door opened. Two children stood in the doorway. The little boy looked to be about five or six, and the girl standing next to him appeared to be slightly younger. Both were dark-haired and dark-eyed, and each of them eyed Luke warily.

''Don't come out here,'' Abigail cautioned. ''We've been using the back door since yesterday,'' she explained to Luke.

''Who is he?'' the little boy asked from the doorway, his voice slightly belligerent.

''Jason, this is Luke Delaney. He's going to build us a front porch that we won't fall through. And Luke, that's Jason and Jessica.''

''Hi, kids.'' Luke smiled at the two rug rats, but neither of them returned his smile. Their dark eyes continued to gaze at him with suspicion.

Luke turned to Abigail. ''I'll get some estimates together and call you with them later this evening.''

''That will be fine,'' she replied and again offered

him that beautiful smile that ignited a small flame in the pit of Luke's stomach.

Yes, it was definitely a good thing Abigail Graham was a married woman with two children, he thought as he nodded goodbye and headed for his pickup truck. Although he found himself incredibly physically attracted to her, the fact that she was married with children assured him he wouldn't follow through on that attraction.

The last thing Luke was looking for was any kind of a permanent relationship. Even if Abigail were single and available, she had that look in her eyes that told him she probably wasn't a short-term-relationship kind of woman.

He dismissed thoughts of the lovely Abigail and her children from his mind as he pointed his pickup toward the family dude ranch.

Adam Delaney, Luke's father, had passed away a little over five months earlier, leaving Luke and his three siblings as heirs to the successful Delaney Dude Ranch. However, Adam Delaney, who had been a mean bastard in life, had kicked his kids one last time in death.

He'd left them the family ranch with a condition attached, that each of them spend twenty-five hours a week working on the ranch for a year. If before that time any one of them defaulted and didn't spend the required time there, the entire estate would transfer to Clara Delaney, Adam's old-maid sister.

Although Luke had no real love for the place where he'd been born and had spent a miserable childhood, he wasn't about to be the one to make his brothers and sister lose their inheritance.

His plans were to remain here in Inferno for another seven months, then when the inheritance was won, he'd sell his interest in the ranch, take the money and chase after his real dream of being a star in Nashville.

And there was no way that dream included a woman, children or anything that remotely resembled a long-term relationship.

"I don't like him." Jason was tucked into bed, the red Kansas City Chiefs sheet pulled up to his stubborn chin. "I don't think he should be here. I don't like the way he looks."

Abby knew who he was talking about, and she also knew it had nothing to do with like or dislike. It had everything to do with fear.

Men frightened both Jason and Jessica ever since that night a year and a month ago…the night their lives had been irrevocably shattered, the night Abby had lost the one person most dear to her heart.

But Abby couldn't think of that. She couldn't dwell on all she'd lost because then she would be lost in grief. She and the kids were in survival mode now, and the only way to survive was to forge ahead and not look back.

"Jason, Luke seemed like a very nice man. I'm sure he won't hurt your sister or you. Besides, we need him. We can't live here if we don't fix the porch."

Jason frowned thoughtfully. "And if he fixes it we can live here together forever?" His dark little eyes pled with her for assurance.

"That's the plan," she replied and leaned forward to kiss his forehead. "Now, go to sleep. We have a big day tomorrow. We've got all kinds of boxes to unpack and maybe tomorrow evening we'll go into town and eat at a restaurant."

"And I can get a chocolate shake?"

Abby laughed. "If the restaurant has them, then you can get one, but now you need to get to sleep."

Dutifully, Jason closed his eyes. After checking to make certain the night-light was burning brightly, Abby shut off the overhead light and left the room.

She went into the smaller bedroom next door where Jessica awaited a night-time kiss. Five-year-old Jessica smiled as Abby entered her bedroom. It was the bright, beautiful smile of a little angel.

"Hi, pumpkin. All tucked in?" Abby sat on the edge of the bed as Jessica nodded. "You didn't eat very much for supper. Are you hungry?"

Jessica shook her head, and Abby wished for the millionth time that she could hear Jessica's voice. Just one word. It had been over a year since the little girl had uttered a word, and Abby could no longer remember what her voice sounded like.

"Good night, sweetheart." Abby kissed Jessica's forehead, checked on her night-light, then left the room.

She went into the kitchen where she poured herself a cup of coffee, then headed for the sofa in the living room. Curling up on one end, with a television sitcom making white noise, she tried to make sense of the million things that were playing in her mind.

School had already begun, and she needed to get

the two kids enrolled, Jason in first grade and Jessica in kindergarten. She hoped the school wouldn't check too deeply into the medical and miscellaneous records needed for enrollment. She'd changed the kids' last name to adhere to their new identity.

She'd done everything she could to cover their tracks, hoped that she'd made no mistakes. Coming here had been a risk, but she'd weighed her options and realized they had no place else to go.

Once the children got settled in school, she'd have to find a job, at least a part-time one. She hoped she could find something that would pay her in cash, where her social security number would not be recorded. She didn't want to leave a trail that somebody might be able to follow.

But eventually a job would become a necessity. It wouldn't be long before their money would be gone, especially with the unforeseen expense of a new porch. It was ironic that there were three trust funds sitting in a bank in Kansas City, each containing enough money to see them living comfortably for the rest of their lives. But she was afraid to access them.

Finding the television noise distracting, she shut it off then went into the kitchen to pour another cup of coffee. She was about to leave the kitchen when the phone rang.

"Mrs. Graham?" a smooth, deep voice inquired.

"Mr. Delaney," she replied, instantly recognizing his voice.

"I've got some figures for you on building a new porch. Is this a good time?"

"Yes, it's fine," she assured him and set her cup on the counter.

As he spoke about the figures and dimensions of the deck, she tried to focus on his words and not on the sexy deepness of his voice. The man had a voice that was positively seductive.

The conversation only took a few minutes. She agreed to the overall price he gave her, and he told her he would have lumber delivered to her home and get started first thing in the morning.

When they hung up, Abby grabbed her coffee cup and headed through the living room and out the front door. Carefully stepping over the hole in the porch, she moved to sit on the rickety steps.

Night had fallen, and the silence was profound. The house was just far enough on the outskirts of Inferno that no city noise was audible. And that was good. The quiet would be good for them all. No ambulance or police car sirens screaming urgency, sounds that always thrust the children into their painful past.

She tilted her head to look at the stars that glittered against the black sky. Instantly she was reminded of Luke Delaney's eyes. His eyes were gray with just enough of a silvery shine and with sinfully black lashes to make them positively breathtaking.

She set her coffee mug aside, wondering if it was the hot brew that was making her overly warm—or thoughts of Luke Delaney.

He'd definitely been a hunk, with his thick, curly black hair and those eyes with their devilish glint. The moment she'd seen him her dormant feminine hormones had whipped into life.

It wasn't just his beautiful eyes, rich dark hair or bold, handsome features that had instantly attracted her. It had also been the lean length of his legs in his tight, worn jeans and the tug of his T-shirt across impossibly broad shoulders.

He'd filled the air with his presence, his scent, his utter masculinity, and he'd reminded her of all the things she'd given up when she'd chosen the path she was on.

She'd hated lying to him, telling him they were from Chicago, but lying was not only necessary, it was positively vital to survival.

She had invented a story for herself that she intended to adhere to. The story was that she was a widow from Chicago who had left the windy city because it held too many painful memories of her husband. A husband who, in reality, had never existed.

Sighing, she wrapped her arms around herself and for just a moment allowed herself the luxury of imagining what it would be like to be held through the night in strong, male arms. She closed her eyes and tried to remember what it felt like to have male lips touching hers in a combustible kiss. Oh, how she used to love to kiss!

She snapped her eyes open, recognizing that she was indulging in a perverse game of self-torture. Those days and nights of Ken were gone, lost beneath family tragedy, lost because he had turned out to be less than half the man she'd believed him to be.

Ken was gone from her life, and there would be no more men for her. The most important things in her life were the two children sleeping in the house where she intended to make a home.

Draining her coffee, she stood and went into the silent house. Although it was still early, she decided to go to bed. Luke had said he'd begin work on the porch early in the morning, and she was exhausted.

She entered her bedroom and stifled a moan as she saw the chaos. Since arriving here, all the unpacking had been done in the kids' rooms, the living room and kitchen. Little had been done in this room.

Boxes were everywhere, and clothes spilled out of an open suitcase on the floor. The only items she'd unpacked were the sheets that were on the bed, her alarm clock that sat on the nightstand and a colorful porcelain hummingbird that was also on the nightstand.

She sank on the edge of the bed and picked up the hummingbird, the delicate porcelain cool beneath her fingertips. It had been a birthday present two years ago, given to her by her older sister.

"You always accuse me of flitting around like a hummingbird," Loretta had said. "So, I figured I'd give this to you and whenever you look at it you can think of me."

Abby's vision blurred with tears as she set the figurine on the nightstand. She couldn't think of Loretta. She didn't have time for grief, didn't have the energy for mourning. The best thing she could do was carry on, remain strong, and that's exactly what she intended to do.

She undressed and got into her nightgown, then turned off the light and slid beneath the sheets. The moonlight poured through the window and painted silvery streaks on the bedroom walls.

The moon seemed much bigger, much brighter here in Inferno, Arizona, like a giant benign night-light chasing away the deepest darkness of the night. She hoped it would keep the bogeyman away.

As always, just before she closed her eyes, she prayed. "Please…please don't let him find us," she whispered fervently. "Please don't let Justin find us."

Justin.

Her personal bogeyman.

The man they'd been running from for the past eleven months. If he found them, then he would destroy them. If he found them, then all would be lost.

Chapter 2

For the thirty-sixth day in a row, Luke woke up stone-cold sober. He opened his eyes and waited for the familiar banging in his head to begin, anticipated the nasty stale taste in his mouth.

Then he remembered. He didn't drink anymore.

He sat on the edge of his bed and looked around. There was no denying it, without the hazy, rosy glow of an alcoholic buzz, the room where he lived in the back of the Honky Tonk looked grim.

The room was tiny and held the battle scars of a thousand previous occupants. It boasted only a single bed, a rickety nightstand and chest of drawers and its own bathroom.

He'd taken the room because he'd wanted to be off the family ranch and because most nights he worked at the Honky Tonk, playing his guitar and singing and, until a little over a month ago, drinking too much.

Until a little over a month ago he'd thought he'd had a perfect life. He'd had his music and he'd had his booze and there had been nights when he hadn't been sure what was more important to him.

It had taken a crazy deputy trying to kill his sister, Johnna, to change Luke's life.

Luke had stumbled into the scene of the almost crime and, had he not immediately beforehand downed a couple of beers, he might have realized Johnna was in trouble. But, with reflexes too slow and a slightly foggy brain, Luke had become a victim, as well. He'd been knocked unconscious, and it had been up to somebody else to save not only Johnna, but Luke, as well.

He'd awakened in the hospital with a concussion and a firm commitment to change his life. He was twenty-nine years old, and it was time to get his life together. And part of that new commitment included no more drinking, and working hard at his carpentry business, buying time until he could leave Inferno behind forever.

But making the choice to change his life and actually doing it were two different things. There wasn't a moment of the day that went by that he didn't want a drink, had to consciously fight the seductive call of a bottle of Scotch or whiskey.

He gazed at the clock on the scarred nightstand. After seven. He'd shower, dress and get right out to the Graham place to start work. Old Walt Macullough, who owned the lumberyard, liked to get his deliveries done early, before the infamous Inferno heat peaked midday.

It wasn't until he was standing beneath a hot spray of water that he remembered the dreams he'd had the night before. Crazy dreams…erotic dreams of a dark-haired woman with sexy spring-green eyes.

He adjusted the temperature of the water to a cooler spray as his memories of the dream hiked his body temperature higher. In the dream he and Abigail had been splendidly naked and locked in an intimate embrace.

His fingers tingled with the imaginary pleasure of stroking her silky skin, tangling in her length of rich, thick hair. And in his dream her sexy, husky voice had cried out with pleasure as he'd taken complete and total possession of her.

Crazy. He shut off the water and grabbed a towel, shoving away the sensual imaginings. All the crazy dreams proved only that he'd been incredibly physically attracted to Mrs. Abigail Graham, but he certainly didn't intend to follow through on his attraction. After all, she was a married lady, and Luke had never and would never mess with any woman who was married.

But one thing was certain. Luke loved women. Maybe it was because his mother had died when giving birth to Luke's sister, Johnna. Luke had only been a year old.

He'd been raised by a parade of housekeepers, most of whom had stayed only for a month or two before being driven away by Luke's father. Adam Delaney had been a son of a bitch, and keeping household help had been a real problem.

The result was that women entranced Luke. He

liked the way they smelled, the feel of their soft skin. He was fascinated by the way their minds worked, but that didn't mean he wanted to bind himself to any woman for anything remotely resembling forever.

Within minutes he was in his truck and headed for the Graham place, pleased to have a big job to keep him busy even though he would have to divide his time between the Graham house and the ranch.

Still, there was nothing Luke liked better than working with his hands. At the family ranch he was in charge of maintenance, mending fences and outbuildings. But what he loved the most was cabinetry work, taking a piece of wood and transforming it into a piece of furniture.

Macullough had already been there, Luke discovered as he parked in front of the ramshackle Graham place. A large pile of supplies had been unloaded by one side of the house.

Before letting Abigail know he'd arrived, Luke walked to the supplies and did a mental checklist, making sure everything he needed had been delivered. In the back of his truck he'd loaded the power tools he knew he would need.

When he was finished with the inventory, he grabbed his bulky toolbox from the truck bed, then approached the front door and knocked. Abigail answered the knock wearing a pink T-shirt and jeans and a warm, inviting smile.

"Mr. Delaney."

"Good morning, and please make it Luke. I just thought I'd tell you that I was here." He tried not to focus on the sweet scent of her that seemed to waft in the air all around him.

"You weren't kidding when you said the lumber-yard would probably be here early," she said as she stepped across the hole in the porch and pulled the door closed behind her. "The truck pulled up at six-thirty this morning. How about a cup of coffee before you get started?"

"No, thanks," Luke replied. "I'd like to get most of this porch torn down before the heat of the day gets too intense. Are your kids still in bed?"

She smiled. "Not hardly. For the most part they're on the same schedule as the sun…up at dawn and in bed at dusk. I've got them unloading boxes in their rooms."

Pink was definitely her color, he silently observed. The T-shirt put the hint of roses in her cheeks and made the green of her eyes appear more intense. He couldn't help but notice the firm thrust of her breasts against the cotton material.

He wondered where her husband was, if he'd already left for work or if it was possible he hadn't yet joined his family in their new home. None of my business, he reminded himself firmly.

"I think probably the best thing to do is once I get this all torn down, I'll nail your front door shut so your children don't forget and try to exit the house this way," he said in an attempt to focus his thoughts on the task at hand. "You said you have a back door you can use to exit and enter the house?"

"Yes, a door in the kitchen, and I think nailing this door shut is a terrific idea. As much as I like to think

I'm always in control of the children, sometimes they escape my radar.'' She flashed him a gorgeous smile that shot an arrow of heat directly into the pit of his stomach. ''Do you have children?''

''Nope. No children, no wife. I'm just footloose and fancy-free.''

She nodded. ''Well, I guess I'll just go inside and let you get to work. Don't hesitate to come on in if you need anything.'' She took a step backward and instantly teetered on the edge of the hole in the wood.

''Whoa,'' Luke exclaimed. He reached out and grabbed her by the upper arms to steady her. Instantly she winced, and he quickly released her. ''I'm sorry. Did I hurt you?'' he asked, wondering if he'd used more force than he'd intended in grabbing her.

''No…no, I'm fine.'' She carefully stepped over the hole and flashed him a quick smile that did nothing to reassure him. ''I'll just be inside if you need anything.'' With those words she disappeared into the house.

Luke expelled a deep breath, trying not to think about the fact that her skin had been as soft, as silky, as he'd imagined in his crazy dreams the night before.

And, in that moment when his hands were on her, he'd felt an unexpected quickening of his pulse, an instantaneous surge of heat rising inside him.

She was definitely a sweet temptation, but Luke had fought against temptation before. Besides, he was certain it was because he'd dreamed about her so intimately the night before that he was slightly unsettled around her this morning. Of course, that didn't explain what on earth had prompted him to dream about the woman.

He pulled a sledgehammer from his truck bed. A little hard physical labor, that's all he needed. With grim determination, he set about pulling down the rotting old porch.

For the next couple of hours, Luke worked nonstop. The sun rose higher in the sky, relentless in intensity. It was just before noon when he decided he needed a tall glass of iced water before doing another lick of work.

He walked around the house and nearly ran into Abigail, who was coming out the back door. "I wondered if I could get a glass of iced water," he said.

"Of course. I was just coming around to ask you if you'd like to eat lunch with us," she replied. "I can't offer you anything extravagant, but if you like ham and cheese sandwiches, you're welcome to eat lunch here."

"Sounds good," he agreed. "Normally, I just take a quick break and drive through someplace for a burger."

"Well, as long as you're working here, I'll be more than happy to provide your lunch."

"Thanks, I appreciate it."

Together they entered the kitchen, and again Luke smelled the sweet, floral scent of her. The children stood near the table. He greeted them, but neither of them returned the greeting.

"If you'd like to wash up while I get the food on the table, the bathroom is the second door on the right down the hallway."

He nodded and left the kitchen. As he went down the hallway to the bathroom, his gaze shot into each of the rooms he passed.

The first room on the right obviously belonged to the little girl. It was decorated in shades of pink, and several dolls were on the bed. The first room on the left was the boy's room, with trucks and cars strewn about and a Kansas City Chiefs bedspread on the bed.

He stepped past the bathroom door to peek at the room at the end of the hallway. A double bed was neatly made up with crisp white sheets, but it was apparent by the stack of boxes that unpacking the children's things had taken priority over Abigail and her husband's creature comforts.

Luke liked that. There had been a time in his life when he'd desperately wished he'd been a priority in any adult's life. It was good and right that parents thought of their children first.

Aware he was out of line peeking into the room, he hurried into the bathroom. The only soap he could find was a bar in the shape of a cartoon character that smelled of bubble gum.

He quickly washed his hands and face, then returned to the kitchen where Abigail was busy pulling things out of the refrigerator and the two kids were setting the table.

His gaze swept around the kitchen. He noted the wooden cabinets looked nearly as weak and rotted as the front porch. The floor was covered with linoleum that was ripped and faded.

"As you can see, we need some work done inside, as well," she said, apparently noting where his gaze had lingered. "When Jason's foot went through the porch, getting it fixed was a priority. Sturdy cabinets are next on my list. Please, have a seat." She gestured him to the table.

"I really appreciate this, Abigail," he said.

She flashed him one of her gorgeous smiles. "Oh, please call me Abby," she said as he slid into a chair.

Abby. Yes, it suited her far better than the more formal Abigail. Luke sat at the end of the table, and the two children silently slipped into the chairs on either side of him.

He'd never seen two kids so quiet, nor had he ever seen kids with such shadows in their eyes. He thought of the black eye Abby had sported the day before, a black eye that was less visible today. That, coupled with the unchildlike behavior of the kids, caused a knot to twist in Luke's stomach.

He knew all about child abuse. His father hadn't thought twice before backhanding, punching or kicking his kids. The Delaney children had been quiet, too. Quiet and careful, with dark shadows in their eyes.

He frowned and tried to dismiss these thoughts, aware that his own background and experience were probably coloring how he was perceiving things. Besides, thoughts of his father always triggered an unquenchable thirst for a drink of something far stronger than water.

Abby set several more items in the center of the table, then sat across from him. "Please, don't stand on ceremony. Just help yourself."

Luke complied, taking a couple slices of bread and building himself a sandwich. He added a squirt of mustard, then turned and smiled at the little girl next to him. "Jessica, you need some mustard on that?"

"She doesn't talk," Jason exclaimed. "She doesn't talk to anyone 'cept me. She won't talk to you 'cause she doesn't like you."

"Jason," Abby reprimanded softly. Luke looked at the young boy in surprise.

"She probably doesn't like me because she doesn't really know me yet. But once she gets to know me, she'll find out I'm quite lovable." He winked at Jessica, who quickly stared at her plate.

"You know, I noticed this morning when I was checking out the lumber in the yard that there's a big old tree in the backyard that looks like it would be perfect for a tire swing," Luke continued.

"A tire swing?" Jason eyed him with a begrudging curiosity.

"Yeah, you know, a tire on a rope that you can climb in and swing on," Luke explained.

Jason gazed at him for another long moment then frowned at his plate. "I don't think we'd like that," he finally said, but his voice lacked conviction.

"I'll tell you what, why don't I bring the stuff to make the swing tomorrow, then if you and Jessica want to swing on it that's okay, and if you don't want to, that's okay, as well."

"I don't want you to go to any trouble," Abby said, her gaze warm on him.

He shrugged. "No trouble. It will just take a few minutes to tie a tire to that tree." He smiled at her. "I always wanted a tire swing when I was little, but my father wouldn't let us have one."

Once again Jason looked at him. "Is your daddy mean?" he asked.

"My daddy was the meanest man on the earth," Luke replied truthfully.

"No more questions, Jason. Let Mr. Delaney eat his lunch," Abby said to the child, then turned her gaze once again to Luke. "Would you like some potato salad?"

"Sure. Sounds good."

She half stood to pass the bowl across the table to him. As she stretched out her arm, her T-shirt sleeve rode up, exposing a livid bruise on her underarm.

That's why she'd winced when he'd grabbed hold of her earlier, he thought. He took the bowl from her and spooned a portion on his plate, his mind racing.

A black eye, an ugly-looking bruise…was the lovely Abigail Graham being abused by her husband? The bruises, coupled with Jason asking him if his daddy was mean, caused ugly speculation to whirl inside him.

He tried to tell himself it was none of his business. He tried to tell himself to stay out of it. But the thought of some man angrily putting his hands on the delicate, fragile woman before him, or hurting the children beside him, enraged him.

He set his fork down and looked at her. "Uh… could I speak with you for a moment out in the living room?"

She gazed at him curiously, then wiped her mouth with her napkin. "Sure," she agreed. She stood and looked at the kids. "You guys go ahead and keep eating. We'll be right back."

Luke allowed her to precede him into the living room. "Is something wrong?" she asked, a worried frown appearing on her forehead as she turned to face him.

"I don't know. You tell me." Luke drew a deep breath, aware that he was about to invade deep into her personal territory. "I know this is really none of my business, but does your husband have a problem?" he finally blurted.

Her eyes widened in obvious surprise. "What do you mean?"

"I couldn't help but notice that you have the evidence of a black eye and a big bruise on your arm." Luke gazed at her intently. "What I really need to know is if you need some help."

Abby stared at the big, handsome man before her and swallowed hard against the tears that suddenly pressed at her eyes. Help? She needed help in a thousand different ways, but certainly not in the way he meant.

"There is no husband," she confessed. Shock swept over his features. "There's no abusive husband, no abusive boyfriend. I'm a widow, and now it's just the kids and me and I can be incredibly clumsy at times." The lie tripped smoothly off her tongue but left a bitter taste in her mouth.

She wasn't sure he believed her, but her heart expanded with warmth that he'd cared enough to ask. She offered him what she hoped was a reassuring smile. "This moving business has been far more physical than I anticipated. A box fell off a shelf and hit

me in the eye, and I'm not sure how I got the bruise
on my arm. But we're getting settled in enough that
bumps and bruises are at an end.''

She reached out and touched his forearm, trying not
to notice the hard muscle beneath the warmth of his
skin. ''But thank you for asking.'' Self-consciously
she dropped her hand.

''I just had to make sure nobody was hurting you.''

Abby nodded, finding the fact that he cared far too
appealing. ''Nobody is hurting me, so that's that.
We'd better go finish our lunch.''

He nodded, and together they returned to the table.
The meal was finished in relative silence, and Abby
was grateful when the food was once again put away,
Luke was back at work, and she could escape to her
bedroom to finish unpacking.

It had been slightly disconcerting to sit at the table
across from him and feel the silvery gray glow of his
eyes on her. She was far more aware of him than she
should be.

She pulled her bedspread from a box and opened it
up to air out. The room would feel more like her own
with her sunflower spread on the bed and her favorite
knickknacks and perfumes on the dresser top.

She had peeked in on Jessica and Jason before coming into her room and knew they were having a pretend picnic on the floor in Jason's room. As usual,
Jason was doing all the talking, but occasionally she
heard a girlish giggle from Jessica, and the sound
warmed her heart.

As she worked unloading the last of the boxes, she
heard the sound of banging coming from the porch.

For a moment she allowed her mind to visualize Luke swinging the sledgehammer. She could vividly imagine the play of the firm muscles in his arms and across his back. Her fingers tingled as she remembered the warmth of his skin beneath her touch.

From the moment she'd told him she was a widow, she'd sensed a subtle change in him. He seemed less standoffish, smiling at her with a gleam in his eyes that made her breath catch in her chest.

She shook her head, as if to dislodge the thoughts. The last thing she could do was invite a man into any area of her life. She was living a lie, and to allow anyone in meant the possibility of danger and heartbreak.

It was nearly an hour later that she heard the sound of the back door opening and closing and knew Luke had entered the kitchen. She left her bedroom and hurried into the kitchen just in time to see him gulping a glass of water.

"Whew, it's definitely warm out there," he said.

Abby nodded, trying to keep her focus on his face. At some point he had taken off his shirt, and his broad, tanned chest shimmered with a light sheen of perspiration. The dark, springy hair that sprinkled his chest formed a valentine pattern, the faint tail disappearing into the waistband of his low-slung tight jeans.

She suddenly realized he was looking at her expectantly as if waiting for her to say something, and a flush of heat warmed her cheeks. She leaned against the table, hoping he hadn't noticed her intense perusal of his firmly muscled, gorgeous chest. "I meant to ask you, I'm going to take the kids out to dinner tonight, but we haven't been in town to really see what's there. Any suggestions on a good place to eat?''

He set the glass on the counter and swiped a hand through his beautiful thick hair. "My personal choice is the diner on Main Street. It's nothing fancy, but the food is good, and it's where most everyone in town eats."

"With two kids, I'm not in the market for fancy. Do they have chocolate shakes?"

He grinned at her, that wide, sexy grin that did amazing things to his sinfully gorgeous eyes. "Do I feel the kinship of another chocolate shake addict?"

"Not me," she protested with a laugh. "Jason is a chocoholic. I prefer anything with strawberries."

"Hmm, the best way to eat strawberries is lying down on a blanket beneath a big old shade tree." His gaze seemed to hold the glint of blatant flirtation. "And they taste best of all when somebody else is feeding them to you, rather than you eating them by yourself."

"I wouldn't know about that," she said, her insides trembling at the picture he'd painted with his words. "I've never had anyone feed me anything."

"That's an oversight that will have to be addressed," he replied. He studied her for a long moment. "You mentioned earlier that you're a widow. How long has it been?"

There was a gentleness in his voice that made her regret the lies she was about to tell. "A little over a year. He died in a car accident."

"I'm sorry. It must have been tough for you and the kids."

She nodded and averted her gaze from his. She didn't want to see the sympathy there, sympathy for a dead husband who had never existed. "We've managed okay on our own."

"Yeah, well, if you ever need a man around here, you know, to do any heavy lifting or whatever, don't hesitate to call me."

She looked at him again, and something in his metal-flecked eyes made her feel as if he were offering her more than strong arms to lift heavy items. Her cheeks burned with a blush as she wondered if perhaps she was reading more into his offer than he'd intended.

"Thanks, I'll keep that in mind."

"If you really want to eat at the diner, I recommend you go around five. By six the place is packed on most evenings, but Friday night is always the worst."

She nodded, then turned and headed out the kitchen door. She drew a deep breath as she entered her room, wondering why a man she hadn't exchanged more than a hundred words with affected her so. Maybe it was because the sight of him evoked thoughts and images that had little to do with conversation.

"Jason," she said as she entered his room. "Time for a bath, buddy."

"A bath? But it's not bedtime," he protested.

"If I'm taking my best boy into town for dinner, then I want him scrubbed sparkly clean." His face screwed up for another round of protest. "And I hear the place we're going to eat has the most super-duper chocolate shakes in the world." The promise of his favorite drink did the trick, and he headed for the bathroom.

Within minutes Abby had Jason in the tub with Jessica waiting to bathe next. Abby had just pulled Jason from the tub and was fixing fresh water for Jessica when Luke appeared in the doorway.

"Sorry to bother you," he said, "but I'm going to nail the front door shut, then knock off for the day."

She quickly turned off the faucets, gestured Jessica to get in the tub, then stepped into the hallway and pulled the bathroom door closed behind her to afford the little girl her privacy.

The first thing she realized was that the hall seemed far too small. He stood close enough to her that she could smell the masculine scent of him, a mixture of fresh cologne and a whisper of hot male. The heat from his body radiated outward. "You'll be back tomorrow?" she asked.

"Yeah, but before I leave, I wanted to talk to you for a minute about my hours here."

She wanted to move him out of the hallway, step back enough from him that she didn't feel so vulnerable, so overwhelmed by his presence.

"If it's all right with you, I'll work here each day until about three. Then I need to knock off. I work on the family ranch in the afternoons, then in the evenings I work at the Honky Tonk, a little bar on the edge of town."

"Three jobs? You must be an overachiever."

He laughed, a deep, rumbling sound that echoed in the pit of his stomach. "Not hardly. In fact, most people would tell you the opposite is true, that I'm just kind of drifting through life, dabbling here and there."

"And what would be closer to the truth?" she asked curiously.

"I'm not sure. I'm still trying to figure it out," he admitted with a wry grin. He started down the hallway toward the kitchen, and she followed.

"I'll be back around seven in the morning," he said as he reached the door.

"That would be fine," she agreed.

"Then I'll see you first thing in the morning." With another of his beautiful smiles, he turned and left the house.

To Abby, his parting words felt like a nice promise, and that worried her. She closed the door after him and for a moment leaned against it.

What was wrong with her? Why did Luke Delaney make her feel so shaky inside, so vulnerable and needy? And why did she have the feeling that once he'd discovered she wasn't married, he'd been subtly flirting with her?

She knew exactly what was wrong with her and knew she couldn't trust her own perceptions. For the first time in a little over a year, she was feeling relatively safe, anticipating the beginning of a normal life…a new beginning.

For a moment, as Luke had looked at her with his flirting gray eyes, she'd been taken back in time, back to a time of innocence, before tragedy had taken its toll.

She responded to Luke because for the first time in a very long time she felt the stir of wonderful, frightening hope. But she knew how quickly hope could be destroyed, how fast lives could shatter. She knew better than to hope for anything.

Chapter 3

Abby and the children had driven into Inferno the day they had arrived for a brief visit to the grocery store, but this was their first real foray into town.

As far as Abby was concerned, it was a delightful little town, with a main street typical of hundreds of other small towns across the United States.

When they'd been driving from Kansas City, Missouri, to Inferno, they'd gone through dozens of towns just like this one, and each time Abby had thought how nice it would be to call one of those small towns home.

The businesses were all in one- or two-story buildings, and each had a charming facade that spoke of what lay inside. The barbershop had an actual barber pole just outside its doors, and the floral shop had two barrels of wildly blooming flowers. The sidewalks were wide and shaded with small trees planted here and there.

It was just after five when she pulled her car into a parking spot directly in front of the Inferno Diner. The kids tumbled out of the back seat as Abby stepped out of the car. In the past month, the kids had grown accustomed to diners in small towns.

Stepping inside the establishment, Abby sniffed appreciatively. The air spoke of good home cooking and strong black coffee. She gestured the kids into a booth near the jukebox, knowing they would eventually end up there, feeding coins to the brightly lit machine to hear songs they didn't know.

"I want a cheeseburger, French fries and a chocolate shake," Jason pronounced as they got seated.

Abby nodded and looked at Jessica, who sat next to her brother in the red plastic booth. "What about you, sweetheart?"

Jessica shrugged.

"How about a grilled cheese sandwich with fries and a soda?" Abby suggested, knowing it was the little girl's favorite. Jessica nodded.

"Hi folks." An older woman with gray hair and a big smile greeted them and handed Abby a menu. "The special today is meat loaf, but I highly recommend you steer clear away from it."

Abby laughed. "Thanks for the honesty."

The waitress grinned. "The cook here does just about everything to perfection, but there's something scary about his meat loaf." She tilted her head and eyed Abby. "You just passing through, or one of the dude ranch guests, or are you new in town?'' the woman asked with unabashed curiosity.

"We've just moved into the old Graham place on the edge of town," Abby replied.

"Whooee, you've sure got your work cut out for you. By the way, I'm Stephanie...Stephanie Rogers, head waitress of this fine establishment."

"Abby Graham. The local space alien was a great-uncle of mine."

Stephanie laughed, a loud, robust sound of one accustomed to laughing often. "Ah, honey, every family has at least one in their family. I've got a brother we all try not to claim because he's nuttier than a fruitcake." The laughter in her blue eyes faded and she looked at Abby seriously. "But that old Graham place is kind of a wreck."

"It isn't as bad on the inside as it looks on the outside," Abby replied. "Besides, I've already hired a carpenter to work on the place...Luke Delaney. Do you know him?"

Stephanie rolled her eyes. "Honey, every woman in the four-state area knows Luke Delaney." She leaned closer to Abby. "That man is sin walking on two legs." Her gaze flickered to the children. "Course, if you're married, then you're safe."

"I'm widowed," Abby replied.

"Then you'd better watch yourself. That handsome devil drips charm from every pore in his body, and he can seduce a woman before she knows what's happened."

Stephanie used her order pad to fan her face.

"There are days when I see him and wish I wasn't so long in the tooth and could have a go at him."

"At the moment all I want from him is a new front porch," Abby replied with a laugh, although she was more than a little unsettled by Stephanie's characterization of Luke.

"Famous last words," Stephanie replied with a wry grin. "Now, what can I get for you all?"

She took their orders and small talked a moment longer, then left the booth and disappeared into the kitchen area.

"Can we have money for the jukebox?" Jason asked.

"Not until after we eat," Abby replied. "You know the rule, eat first, play the jukebox afterward." It was a rule she'd instigated the first time she and the kids had eaten at a place that had a jukebox.

She'd mistakenly allowed them to play songs before their meals were served and had had to fight with them to get them in their seats to eat.

Before Jason could lodge any real protest, Stephanie returned to their table with their beverages. A thick chocolate shake effectively stilled any complaint Jason might have uttered.

"Cute kids," Stephanie said as she lingered for a moment at their table.

"Thanks, I think so," Abby replied.

"What's your name, cutie?" Stephanie asked Jessica.

Jessica's gaze instantly went to her brother. "She doesn't talk," he explained soberly. "She doesn't talk to anyone but me."

"Shy, huh. My oldest boy was like that," Stephanie said to Abby. "He's twenty-five now and still doesn't talk much unless he's got something really important to say."

"Hey, Stephanie, how about some fresh coffee over here," a guy hollered from the counter.

"No rest for the wicked," she said with a wink, then hurried away.

Abby took a sip of her soda and settled back in the seat. She wished it were just shyness that kept Jessica silent. But she knew it was much more than that, and it ached inside her that after a whole year Jessica still didn't trust Abby enough to speak to her, that the little girl trusted and depended solely on her brother.

Within a few minutes, Stephanie had served them their meals and they were all eating. It was only then that Abby allowed the conversation with the waitress to replay in her mind.

Sin walking on two legs. Yes, that was certainly an apt description, at least physically, of Luke Delaney. From the moment she'd seen him standing at her doorstep, with those gorgeous eyes and that drop-dead lean body with his mountain-broad shoulders, she'd been affected on a purely hormonal level.

But Stephanie's words warned Abby away from what she knew would be foolishness in any case. She could not get involved with any man, not yet...not until she knew for certain they were safe and her secrets were secure.

Even if she was in the market for a relationship with a man, the last kind of man she wanted was a handsome charmer with seduction on his mind.

If and when she decided to invite a man into her life, it would be a man who had the capacity to parent two wounded children, a man who could be a source of strength, support and love for Abby. She certainly didn't need a good-looking cowboy carpenter with a reputation of being a ladies' man.

As they ate, the diner began to fill with people, and Abby was glad she'd taken Luke's advice and come early enough to beat what appeared to be a dinner rush in the making.

She felt the curious gazes of other diners on her and the kids and knew that probably strangers in town were a topic for gossip. It wouldn't be long and everyone would know she was Inferno's newest resident, and not just a passerby who had stopped in for a meal.

"How about some dessert?" Stephanie asked when they had finished the meal. "I've got a fresh apple pie back there that's still warm from the oven."

Abby looked at the kids, who both shook their heads. "I'll take a piece, and a cup of coffee," she said, deciding she could enjoy the pie and coffee while the kids played the jukebox.

Minutes later, the kids stood at the music maker armed with a handful of quarters, and Abby nursed her coffee and cut into the luscious-looking apple pie.

She'd just taken her first bite when Luke Delaney walked into the diner. Instantly, she felt as if the air pressure in the room subtly increased.

He paused inside the door, his long-lashed eyes scanning the room. When his gaze landed on her, a slow smile curved his lips. As he sauntered toward her, she was aware of every other woman in the room watching his progress.

He stopped at her table and smiled. "I see you got here okay." He flickered his gaze to the empty space beside her. "Mind if I join you?"

She wanted to tell him no but found herself scooting as close to the wall as possible to allow him plenty of room to sit next to her.

"Stephanie." He raised a hand to the waitress. "Bring me the usual." The waitress nodded, and Luke slid into the booth next to Abby. "Where are the munchkins?" he asked.

She pointed to the jukebox near the door where the two were feeding in coins and punching buttons. "On the cross-country drive they discovered the joys of the jukebox," she said.

"Do they know what they're playing? I mean, can they read the titles?"

"Jason can read a little, enough to recognize all the Alan Jackson songs."

He laughed. "At least the kid has good taste in music."

"You like country music?" she asked, trying to ignore the clean male scent of him that seemed to wrap around her so effectively. His body warmth seeped to her even though their bodies weren't touching.

He turned sideways so he could look at her, his thigh suddenly pressing against hers. "As far as I'm concerned, there's no other kind of music. What about you? What's your listening pleasure?"

She tried to focus on what he was saying and not on the sensory overload of his nearness. Despite the material of his jeans and hers, she could feel the heat of his thigh intimately against her own. "I used to enjoy old rock and roll, but when we were driving across country, there were times when we could only pick up country stations, so I have to admit, I've grown pretty fond of it."

"You should come down to the Honky Tonk one night."

"The Honky Tonk?" She was intensely aware of speculative glances being shot their direction from the other diners, particularly the female diners.

"It's a little tavern on the north side of town. I pick a little guitar and sing there most nights."

"Really? So you're a singing carpenter cowboy rancher."

"Yeah, although I'm hoping eventually I can drop carpenter cowboy rancher from my résumé."

She looked at him in surprise. "So, you want to be a performer?" He was certainly handsome enough. She wondered if he had any talent, other than the one of seduction that Stephanie had mentioned earlier.

"In seven months' time I'm Nashville bound," he said, his eyes sparkling with good humor. "And in the meantime, I've got a front porch to build."

She returned his smile with one of her own. "Why seven months? I mean, if Nashville and fame are your dream, then why wait to chase after it?"

Abby knew all about the danger of waiting to reach for dreams. She knew that far too often if you waited too long, fate destroyed any chance of gaining the dreams you might entertain. No, fate hadn't destroyed her dreams, Justin Cahill had seen to that.

She shoved this thought aside and listened as Luke explained to her about his father's will. "Anyway, the short of it is that if I don't want my brothers and sister to lose their inheritance, then I have to hang around here for the next seven months and put in twenty-five hours a week at the family ranch."

He grinned, that slow, lazy smile that ignited heat in the pit of her stomach. "But, with a new pretty lady in town, hanging around here isn't going to be so bad, after all."

"I already warned her about you, Luke Delaney." Stephanie placed a dinner platter before him and eyed him in mock sternness. "I told her to watch out for you, that you're a charming devil without a heart."

Luke laughed and turned to Abby. "Don't pay any attention to her. She knows the only reason I don't have a heart is because she stole it from me long ago." He turned to look at the waitress. "You know you're the only woman for me, Stephanie."

She slapped him on the shoulder with her order pad. "And you are utterly shameless. You drink too much, you don't take care of yourself and you never take anything seriously." With these words and a wry shake of her head, she turned and left their table.

"She always gives me a hard time," he explained, his features still lit with humor.

"She did warn me about you before you got here," Abby replied. "She said you were a charmer." Abby bit her bottom lip, unwilling to tell him what Stephanie had said about his powers of seduction.

Luke looked at her once again, and she wondered

if he had any idea that his eyes seduced by merely gazing at her. "And that's a bad thing?"

"Well, no..." She felt breathless beneath the power of his bedroom eyes. "That is, unless the woman you're charming takes you too seriously."

He grinned. "I take my charming of women very seriously."

She broke the eye contact with him and gazed to where the two kids stood at the jukebox, tapping their feet and wiggling their bottoms in the unself-consciousness of children.

He didn't speak until she looked at him once again, then he smiled that sexy grin that released a million butterflies in the pit of her stomach. "I'll tell you what, I'll give you fair warning before I attempt to charm you, and that way you won't be caught unprepared."

Despite the fact that Abby felt as if she had suddenly plunged into deep waters over her head, she laughed. "Okay," she agreed. "That sounds fair to me." Once again she broke their eye contact and looked at the kids. "And now, if you'll excuse me, it's time for me to get home and get those two ready for bed."

In actuality, it was time for her to get away from Luke Delaney's smile, his body warmth and the heated light that shone from his eyes. He was making her feel things she hadn't felt for a very long time.

She sighed in relief as he stood to allow her to slide out of the booth. "I guess I'll see you in the morning," she said.

"Bright and early," he replied, and in his smooth,

deep voice she heard promise that had nothing to do with a new front porch.

She nodded, turned and walked to the cash register, refusing to follow her impulse to turn and look at him one last time.

The man was a definite temptation, but she knew the temptation he offered was not what she needed or wanted in her life at the moment. He could try his talent at seduction with her, but what he would eventually discover was that at this point in her life, she was absolutely, positively unseduceable.

Luke had been in a tailspin ever since learning that Abigail Graham had no husband and no boyfriend. It was as if fate had given him the thumbs-up to follow through on his initial attraction to her.

There was nothing Luke liked more than a challenge and the excitement of a new, fresh relationship. It had been several months since he'd even taken a woman on a date and months before that when he'd last been intimate with a woman.

He knew he had a reputation as a womanizer, and in truth had dated most of the single, eligible women in town. But since his father's death, Luke had not been living up to his reputation.

As he ate, he thought about the lovely Abby, whose clean, lightly floral perfume still eddied in the air around him. A year was a long time to be alone, and there had been loneliness in her eyes, a loneliness that touched something deep inside him.

He shook his head as if to dislodge this thought. He certainly wasn't lonely. His life was merely in a holding pattern until the seven months he had to spend at the ranch were over. And there was no reason he shouldn't spend some of his holding-pattern time with a lovely woman named Abigail Graham.

By the time he'd finished his meal, the dinner rush had come and gone. Stephanie poured herself a cup of coffee and sank down across from him in the booth.

"I shouldn't even talk to you," Luke teased with an affectionate grin at Stephanie. "What are you doing maligning my good name behind my back to the new people in town?"

Stephanie snorted. "You don't need any help maligning your name. I told that pretty lady the truth, that she needs to watch out for you. You're a heartbreaker, Luke Delaney, and you've already broken half the hearts in this town."

"But I'm good friends with every single woman I've ever dated," he countered.

"And that's part of your charm, dear Luke. You somehow manage to make every woman happy they got a moment of your time even though they wanted a lifetime."

Stephanie took a sip of her coffee and shook her head with a smile. "But, mark my words, Luke. Someday you're going to mess with the wrong woman and you'll have one of those obsessive stalkers on your hands like in the movies."

Luke laughed in genuine amusement. "Ah, Stephanie, you always did have a flair for the dramatic. I'm twenty-nine years old and I'm not cut out for marriage or family life. I play fair and make sure all the women I date know that ahead of time."

Stephanie waved her hands to dismiss his statement. "If anyone in this town wasn't cut out for marriage, it was your sister, Johnna. And look at her now, the picture of happily married bliss." Stephanie finished her coffee and stood. "All you need Luke, is one good woman to tame you and you're finished."

Luke laughed, certain that no woman was ever going to tame and domesticate him. "Trust me, Stephanie. Growing up in my family gave me all the family experience I ever want in my life."

Stephanie frowned. "You can't judge marriage and family by what your daddy did to you kids. Every man needs a good woman, Luke. And that's exactly what you need in your life." With these final words, Stephanie turned and left his booth.

Luke sipped his coffee, thinking of Stephanie's words. It had always amazed him that everyone in town seemed to know what a mean, hateful son of a bitch Adam Delaney had been as a father, but nobody had ever stepped in to help the four children who suffered at his hands.

He shoved away thoughts of his father. Thinking of Adam Delaney always caused a knot of fire to form in the pit of his stomach, a knot that only a good stiff drink could unkink. Instead, he focused on a vision of the lovely Abigail Graham.

Not only did she interest him on a physical level, but she intrigued him, as well. Along with the loneliness he'd thought he'd seen in her eyes, he'd sensed secrets. She certainly hadn't been forthcoming about where they had come from.

Back east, she'd said, then had finally said they

were from Chicago. But, when he had gone past the bedrooms, he'd noticed that Jason's room was decorated in a Kansas City Chiefs motif. Why would a kid from Chicago want items from the Kansas City football team in his room? Why not the Chicago Bears?

Luke sipped the last of his coffee and wondered if perhaps he was making too much of nothing. Maybe the kid's father had been a Chiefs fan, or perhaps he'd had a friend from the Kansas City area who had gotten him to follow the team. In any case, it didn't much matter. He didn't really care where she'd come from.

"More coffee?" Stephanie pulled him from his thoughts.

"No, thanks," he replied, and reached in his back pocket for his wallet. "I've got to get out of here. I need to get out to the ranch for a couple of hours before I head over to the Honky Tonk."

"Tomorrow is my night off, and I already told Tom that I want to go to the Honky Tonk and have a drink and listen to you croon a few tunes."

Luke grinned at the older woman. "You and Tom come in, and your first round of drinks is on me." He tossed enough money on the table to pay for his meal and a generous tip.

"Then for sure we'll be in," she agreed.

Luke left the diner, climbed into his pickup and within minutes was headed to the family ranch. He'd surprised himself by telling Abby of his plans to head to Nashville. That was something he hadn't shared with anyone, not even his siblings, who he knew probably didn't give a damn what he did or where he went.

To say the Delaney heirs weren't tightly knit was an understatement.

Still, he had a feeling he'd told Abby his plans for a reason. He was interested in her, but he certainly wasn't interested in anything long-term. By telling her that in seven months his plans were to leave Inferno and never look back, he'd subtly told her that he wasn't a man to pin a future on.

Chapter 4

"How about a glass of iced tea?" Abby asked Luke.

"Sounds great," he agreed. "I'm ready to take a break."

It was late afternoon, and Luke had been working on knocking down the old porch since early morning.

The first thing he had done when he arrived that morning was follow through on his promise to hang a tire swing from one of the thick branches of the tree in the backyard. While the kids had played on the swing, Abby had picked weeds and promised herself to buy a lawnmower in the near future.

She had consciously stayed away from the front of the house where Luke was working.

The heat of the afternoon had finally driven them inside. The kids were playing in their rooms, and Abby had guessed Luke would be ready for a tall drink of something cold.

As Luke put down the sledgehammer, Abby tried to keep her gaze focused everywhere but on his broad, naked chest. She handed him the glass of tea, then stepped back from him and watched as he downed half a glass in long, thirsty gulps.

Condensation from the bottom of the glass dripped onto his chest, and despite her desire to the contrary, she watched the droplet trail down his chest.

"I was hoping I'd be able to salvage some of this wood," he said, and she was grateful for anything that took her attention away from his physique. "But I don't think I'm going to be able to. Most of it is beyond rotten." He took another deep drink, then continued. "I should have the last of this pulled down in the next hour or so, then first thing tomorrow morning I'll start on the new structure."

"It will be nice to be able to walk out the front door and not be afraid of falling through the porch."

"You know, I'd be glad to give you an estimate on some new kitchen cabinets. If I build them from pine, they'd be relatively inexpensive."

"New cabinets would be wonderful," she said thoughtfully. "I've been afraid to put too many canned goods in the ones that are there because they look so weak."

"I'll work up an estimate and you can decide if you want to go ahead then."

"Okay," she agreed, then sighed. "There's so much work here that needs to be done."

"And Rome wasn't built in a day," he replied with one of his killer smiles.

"You're right. And hopefully we'll be here a long time and eventually get the house done the way we want it." She returned his smile with one of her own. "Patience isn't one of my strong suits."

"I've never been one to want to wait for what I want, either," he replied with a wicked grin that instantly drew heat into her cheeks.

He held out his empty glass to her. As she took it from him, their fingers touched and Abby felt a spark of electricity tingle in the air between them. She took another step back from him and clutched the glass tightly in her hand.

There was a silence, an uncomfortable one that she instantly worked to fill. "You mentioned last night at the diner that you had to stay here in Inferno for several months and work on your family dude ranch so your brothers and sisters wouldn't default. So, you have a big family?"

"Two brothers and one sister. And we've recently added a sister-in-law and a brother-in-law." He swiped a hand through his thick hair, and Abby tried not to notice how handsome he looked with the afternoon sun playing on his features.

He had strong, bold features. Midnight dark brows, a straight Roman nose, high cheekbones and a sensual mouth. He was once again clad in customary tight, worn blue jeans that rode low on his hips.

"What about you? Big family? Small family?" he asked.

"No other family. Just me and the kids."

A frown creased his forehead. "I might as well have no family. We aren't very close."

"Do they all live here in town?" she asked curiously.

Luke nodded. "Yeah, Matthew lives at the family homestead. Mark and his wife, April, and son live on a house Mark built on the ranch. Johnna and her husband, Jerrod, live in a house here in town." His frown deepened. "So, we're all here, but we might as well live a million miles away from one another."

"You don't realize how lucky you are to have brothers and a sister," Abby replied. "My sister died a year ago, and there isn't a day that goes by that I don't wish I had spent more time with her, talked to her more often."

As always, thoughts of Loretta brought with them a dark, dangerous well of grief. If only she'd known what had been going on in Loretta's life. If only she'd known the danger. Abby had encouraged her to make the break that had ultimately resulted in her death.

Before Abby could plunge into the dark depths of despair, she mentally shook away thoughts of the sister she missed so much. "Take my advice, Luke and don't waste time where your family is concerned. Enjoy their company while you still have them."

He nodded, his gaze steady, thoughtful as it lingered on her. "So, you lost your sister a year ago. That means you had two tragedies about the same time?"

"Two?" She looked at him blankly.

"Your husband and your sister."

Warmth swept over her as she realized she'd momentarily forgotten all about the husband she'd supposedly lost. "Yes, that's right," she agreed hurriedly, then averted her gaze. "It's been a long, hard year."

He took a step toward her and reached out to grab her hand. She looked at him, surprised by the warmth, the strength of his touch. "I hope Inferno will be good to you and you'll be able to put all the sad times behind you and find happiness here."

For a moment, as she gazed into his beautiful sooty eyes, she wondered if happiness was possible. She hoped so, not so much for her own sake, but for the sake of the two children who meant more to her than anything on the earth.

"Thank you," she replied. She knew she should pull her hand away yet was reluctant to break the warmth and comfort of the contact. It had been so long since she'd felt any kind of masculine touch, even one as simple and uncomplicated as the touch of hands.

He smiled and increased the pressure of his hand on hers. "There's nothing I'd like more than to see those pretty green eyes of yours light up with pleasure, with happiness and laughter."

A dangerous, provocative heat rose inside her as their gazes remained locked, and she saw flickering flames in the depths of his eyes. "Are you trying to charm me, Mr. Delaney?" She forced a light laugh and pulled her hand from his, suddenly realizing his touching her was anything but simple. "Is this the beginning of the seduction that Stephanie warned me about?"

He laughed, a low, sexy rumble that was as disturbing as his touch. "Trust me, darlin', when I start seducing you, you'll know it and you won't have to ask."

His words sent a new flood of heat through her and made the mere act of breathing difficult. "Then trust me, all I really want from you, Luke, is a new front porch and maybe some new kitchen cabinets," she replied quickly, appalled to hear her voice slightly breathless.

Again he laughed. "It's been my experience that women rarely know what they really want."

"And from what Stephanie told me, you certainly have had plenty of experience with women." She shook her head wryly. "Three jobs and an overactive social life. I don't know how you have the strength to get up in the mornings."

Flirting. Someplace in the back of her brain she recognized that's what she was doing. Flirting with Luke Delaney.

He grinned that lazy devastating smile. "My strong suit has always been my terrific stamina."

He laughed as her cheeks grew hot and she knew a blush reddened them. "Besides, my reputation as a womanizer has been greatly exaggerated. You will discover that this town thrives on idle gossip, and I'm not sure why, but I seem to be a favorite topic of that gossip."

Abby certainly knew why. The man was not only as handsome as a pinup model, he had a kind of animal magnetism that she had a feeling could stir the hormones of a female statue.

"So, tell me about your brothers and sister," she said, suddenly desperate to change the topic, get away from the subject of seduction and gossip, neither of which she wanted or needed in her life.

"What do you want to know?" he asked.

"What do they do? What are they like?" She realized she was intrigued by Luke and wondered what kind of family he came from.

"Matthew is the oldest. He's thirty-five and he runs the family dude ranch." Again a frown etched across his forehead. "Matthew is distant and aloof, but he's a good businessman. All that matters to him is the ranch. Mark is thirty-three and he's more easygoing. He's thoughtful and quiet or at least he was until he married April. She's really brought him out of his shell."

The frown disappeared. "Then there is Johnna. She's twenty-eight, a year younger than me." He grinned with obvious affection. "She's stubborn and mule headed, impetuous and opinionated. She's a lawyer who spends most of her time trying to right the wrongs of the world."

"You're close to her," Abby commented.

"I'm closer to her than I am to my brothers, but there's a lot of distance even between me and Johnna."

"Why? I mean, why aren't you and your siblings close?"

He grinned wryly. "What is this? Twenty questions? I don't know the answer to that question." His eyes shadowed slightly. "All I can tell you is that the four Delaney heirs share common parentage, but nothing else. It would take nothing short of a miracle to make us into a real family."

Abby thought she heard a wistful tone in his voice, as if there was a part of him deep inside that longed for a family connection. It echoed inside her, touching a chord of commonality.

Still, as attractive as she found Luke Delaney, she knew she'd be a fool to somehow get the notion into her head that he was the man who could fulfill her dream of a complete and happy family.

Dusk was falling as Luke pulled up in front of the family homestead. He hadn't intended on coming here this evening, but Matthew had called one of the infrequent family meetings, which meant something was amiss.

Luke's stomach tied itself in a knot as he got out of his truck and approached the house where he'd spent the miserable hours and days of childhood.

Family meetings had never been particularly pleasant. Most of the time Matthew called a meeting when something had to be decided, and a final decision among the four very different siblings never came easily.

Each Saturday a late midday meal was served to the guests as a welcome and get-acquainted gathering. But it was late enough in the day that there was no evidence such a gathering had taken place.

The pit fire that cooked burgers and beans had been extinguished, and the tables and chairs put away. The grounds were relatively quiet.

A couple sat at a picnic table beneath a tree, apparently enjoying the sunset that painted the sky in a fiery display of color.

Luke raised a hand in their direction then headed up the stairs to the front door. In two weeks the ranch would go dark for a month. Two months out of the year, one in the spring and one in the fall, the ranch didn't book guests and used the downtime to do major renovation and repair work.

Seven months, Luke reminded himself as he walked in the front door into the airy foyer. Seven months, and then he could leave and never look back. He wouldn't have to worry any more about guests' needs or family dynamics or disturbing memories. He'd blow this place and never look back.

He heard the sound of voices coming from the den and knew that's where the family would be gathered. The knot in his stomach intensified as he stepped into the large room and the first person he saw was Matthew.

As usual, his oldest brother looked as if he'd been chewing on nails. His handsome features were set in a perpetual scowl that evoked in Luke memories of their father.

"Luke." Matthew greeted him with a curt nod.

"Hey, Luke," Johnna said from the love seat where she sat next to her husband, Jerrod. The two of them still had their just-married glow even though their wedding had taken place a little over a month before.

Jerrod had his arm around Johnna, as if she were his most precious possession and he was protecting her from the world at large. Johnna leaned into him, as if in sweet acquiescence. Luke had never seen his sister look as happy as she had in the last month. Marriage to Jerrod definitely agreed with her.

"Would you like a drink?" Matthew asked from the bar in the corner of the room.

Would he like a drink? The siren song rang in his ears, and his mouth grew unaccountably dry. He imagined he could smell Scotch, feel the sweet slide down his throat and the flames as it hit his stomach. Hell, there was nothing he'd like better than a good, stiff drink.

"No, thanks," he forced himself to say, slightly irritated by the question. Shouldn't a brother remember that his brother had quit drinking? "So, where are Mark and April?" he asked as he sat in one of the wing chairs.

"They should be here any time." Matthew carried a drink with him to the chair across from Luke and sat down, the scowl still tugging deep furrows into his forehead.

"Guess what I heard this morning," Johnna said as she shot a coy look at Luke. "I heard that my handsome brother was seen in the diner snuggling up to a new widow woman who has moved into town."

"I wasn't 'snuggling up' to her," he protested with a laugh. "I'm doing some carpentry work out at her place and happened to see her at the diner last night. I was just being neighborly by sitting down with her and visiting for a little bit."

"Who were you being neighborly with?" Mark asked as he and April came into the room.

"The new widow woman who has moved into the old Graham place," Johnna answered. "I heard that she's a real looker, with dark hair and pretty blue eyes."

"Green," Luke corrected. "She has pretty green eyes."

"Better watch out, those green-eyed women will get you every time," Mark said with a loving smile to his dark-haired, green-eyed wife, April.

"If we can dispense with the pleasantries, we've got some work to do," Matthew said.

"By all means, let's dispense with any pleasantries," Luke said dryly. God, he would really love a drink.

There followed an uncomfortable silence as April and Mark settled on the sofa and everyone turned their gaze to Matthew. He finished his drink in one large swallow, then stood and began to pace the length of the multicolored throw rug beneath his feet.

Instantly Luke was thrown back in time, and for a moment he felt as if he were seven or eight years old again and it was his father pacing the floor, working up a head of steam that would result in a beating for one or more of the four kids. Adam Delaney would slam down a shot of bourbon then slam into one of his kids.

He shook his head slightly to dispel the image. Adam Delaney was dead and gone, his only legacy the ranch they had to work to keep and enough dysfunction to keep therapy in fashion for years to come.

"We have several things we need to go over and make decisions about," Matthew began. "First of all, April has been asking me for months about renovating the old barn into a sort of a community building." He turned to April. "You want to explain to them what you have in mind?"

April sat up straighter on the sofa. "You all know that as social director here, I'm always looking for ways to offer the guests exciting and wonderful entertainment. If we renovate the old barn, it will make a terrific permanent place for dances and parties." She looked at Mark as if for reassurance. "I had a contractor come out and look at it and it's structurally sound, but still it's a big investment to make."

"And that's what we need to make a decision about," Matthew said. "In seven months the ranch officially becomes ours. If we're just going to sell it and split the proceeds, then I don't see the point in investing any money in renovating the old barn."

Luke looked at Matthew in shock. It was the first time he'd ever heard Matthew even mention the possibility of selling the place.

"I don't want to sell," Mark said. He looked at Luke, at Matthew, then at Johnna. "This is Delaney land. We belong here. I want to pass my part of this ranch on to Brian…and to the child April is carrying."

Everyone looked at April in surprise. "It's true," she confirmed. "I'm pregnant."

Johnna squealed with excitement and quickly ran over to hug April while the men congratulated Mark on the news.

"So, we know that Mark doesn't want to sell," Matthew said a few minutes later when things had calmed down. "Johnna, what about you?"

She frowned and raked a hand through her boyishly short dark hair. "To be honest, I haven't given it much thought lately. Between my law practice and having to work here twenty-five hours a week, I haven't had much time to think about what the future holds.''

''But you always said you hated it here,'' Luke reminded her. Their mutual dislike for the family homestead had always been a point of commonality between them.

Johnna frowned. ''When Father was alive, I definitely hated this place. Now that he's gone, I'm not sure how I feel.''

''Look,'' Mark interjected. ''Do we really have to make a decision about selling right now? Can't we go ahead and do the renovations on the barn without knowing for sure what we're going to do in seven months time?''

''Is the money for the renovations an issue?'' Johnna asked.

Matthew shook his head. ''No, the ranch is doing very well, and we could pay for the renovations without having to take out a loan.''

Luke fought a wave of frustration. He didn't want to put any more money in the ranch. More than anything he wanted to convince his brothers and sister that the best thing for all of them was to sell the ranch in seven months, split the proceeds from the sale, then get on with their own separate lives.

He wanted no ties to this place of unhappiness. He didn't give a damn what the others did. The day the year was up Luke intended to sell his share either to one of his brothers or sister, or to an outsider.

With the decision made to go ahead with the renovations, the family meeting broke up. The four of them rarely spent time in idle chatter. They had no idea how to perform the small talk that would encourage a deepening of their relationship with each other.

Luke was the first to leave. After saying goodbye to everyone, he left the house and headed for his workshop in one of the outbuildings.

He didn't have to be at the Honky Tonk until ten and decided he'd work an hour or so on a rocking chair he'd been making. The workshop was the one place he loved on the ranch. Housed in one end of the stables, it smelled of fresh hay, horses and wood chips. Every tool he'd ever need to transform raw wood into useful and decorative items was at his fingertips, bought with money he'd earned at the Honky Tonk.

The rocking chair was complete except for the sanding and finishing, and as he picked up a piece of sandpaper and got to work, his mind whirled with thoughts of his family.

The Delaney children had learned at an early age not to trust one another. Adam Delaney's parenting skills had included a divide-and-conquer mentality. He'd taught his children to trust nobody—particularly each other.

Often before a beating Luke had been told that his transgression had been brought to Adam's attention by one of his siblings.

Luke and his brothers and sister had remained isolated through misery and fear, and now that Adam was dead, none of them seemed to know how to breach those early years of distance and mistrust.

"Luke?" He jumped in surprise as Mark and April appeared at the doorway of his workshop.

"Hey, what's up?" he asked curiously.

"We just thought we'd stop in before heading back to our place," Mark said.

"What a beautiful chair," April exclaimed.

Luke eyed the two of them in suspicion. They had never been in his workshop area before, and he couldn't imagine what had prompted this unexpected visit. "Thanks."

"I saw one of your coffee tables the other day at Susan Milford's house," April said. "You do such beautiful work, Luke."

He grinned, suddenly realizing a possible reason for their being here. "Let me guess, you want me to make you a crib. Sure, I'll be glad to do it."

"Oh, Luke, that would be wonderful, but that's not the reason we stopped." April smiled at Mark, as if to encourage him. "Go on, ask him."

Mark was obviously ill at ease as he looked first at his wife, then at Luke. "Well, you know April is pregnant," he began. Luke nodded. "Since we found out, she and I have been talking and...well...we'd like you to be the baby's godfather."

Luke stared at his brother and sister-in-law in stunned silence. "Is this a joke?" He couldn't imagine why they would want him to hold such an exalted position in the life of their child. Being a godparent was certainly nothing to take lightly.

"Of course it's not a joke," April replied with a sweet smile. "Mark and I both agree that you would make a wonderful godfather. We both know that beneath your superficial charm and bad-boy reputation is the heart of a loving, caring man, the kind of man we want in the life of our child."

Her words caused an unsettling ball of emotion to well up inside Luke, and he instantly swallowed. He didn't want this.

How could he be a good godparent and leave Inferno in seven months? He didn't want chains holding him here, and this felt like an emotional chain of mammoth proportions.

He swallowed again and cleared his throat. "I really appreciate the thought, but maybe it would be better if you asked Matthew."

Luke saw the disappointment in his brother's eyes and instantly regretted his words. But it wouldn't be fair to the baby to have a godparent who wasn't here to share life experiences.

"Okay," Mark said. "Then I guess we'll ask Matthew." He turned on his heels and left the workroom.

April looked at Luke one last time, confusion wrinkling her delicate brow. "You Delaneys are the most complicated people I know," she said, then turned and followed her husband out the door.

In the ensuing silence, Luke got back to work, trying not to think of what had just occurred. The idea that April and Mark would want him as a godfather still stunned him.

For the first time in his life, Luke felt as if his brother had been reaching out to him, trying to make a connection beyond the superficial one they had shared all their life.

And he'd rejected it. And apparently he'd rejected it badly. Luke sank down on a bench and raked a hand through his hair. If he'd wanted a drink before, he desperately needed one now. All he had to do was walk into the house and help himself to the bar stock Matthew kept on hand. A few drinks, and the pain in his chest would disappear.

Yeah, right, he thought dryly. His pain might go away but he'd be back on the treadmill that led to nowhere. He'd drink himself into the loser his father had always told him he was.

April's words replayed in his mind. She was a sweet woman but obviously seeing characteristics that weren't there. Beneath his superficial charm and bad-boy reputation wasn't much of anything else. And he was not a good bet for a godfather. Matthew would be a much better choice.

He drew a deep breath and thought of his siblings. His brothers and sister were fools for wanting to keep this ranch alive, for being sentimental enough to want to hang on to a place where they'd endured nothing but heartache.

He was the smart one, the strong one who intended to get away. He had a hunger to be somebody, to make something of himself, if only to prove his father wrong.

Funny, each and every one of the Delaney children had suffered physical and mental abuse at the hands of their father, and the experience had made them who they had been as children and who they had become as adults. His siblings were hanging on here in an attempt to be something they would never be…a normal, happy family.

Luke didn't intend to waste his time or energy on

such a fruitless endeavor. Seven months, he told himself. He had seven months here, and then he'd put the past and the bad memories of this place behind him and he'd never, ever look back.

And in the meantime, he had a delightful diversion to occupy his mind for the next seven months. A delightful diversion with dark hair and bright green eyes, a diversion named Abby.

A smile curved his lips as he thought of how delicate and warm her hand had been beneath his earlier that day. And even though she'd told him all she wanted from him was a new front porch, the slight tremor in her voice, the look in her eyes had told him she wasn't as unaffected by him as she'd like him to think.

She knew his reputation, knew his plans to leave Inferno, so she would know exactly what he was offering her and that it had nothing to do with anything long-term.

Yes, indeed, if he had to stick around Inferno for another seven months, it was nice to know that gave him seven months with the winsome Abigail Graham.

Charming a woman was certainly less complicated than family ties and emotional baggage.

Chapter 5

Abby was on edge. She'd been on edge for the past two days while Luke had been working to complete the front porch, but nothing like what she was feeling this afternoon.

She told herself her intense anxiety was due to the fact that early that morning she'd taken the kids to school and enrolled them, then had left them there and returned home alone. She told herself she was worried about how they would fare, that she was afraid the school officials might discover the children weren't named Graham after all and that she was not really their mother.

Although Jessica had been enrolled in an afternoon kindergarten class, Abby had made arrangements for her to attend a morning play group at the school, as well, and she was worried how the little girl would do without her brother for support.

But the truth of the matter was she was nervous because this was the first time she'd been alone in the house while Luke worked outside. And much of her nervousness was due to the fact that he seemed to be aware of their utter aloneness, as well.

He was in and out of the house more often for drinks of water than on any day previous, and whenever she joined him there, he lingered longer than necessary.

He'd arrived just after nine, and after working only a few minutes had asked where the children were. She'd explained that they had started their first day of school, and from that moment on there had been an overt tension between them that simmered in the air.

It was about two-thirty in the afternoon when he told her that he was taking a break from the porch work and wanted to measure the kitchen cabinets and could use her help.

"It's much easier to get measurements with another person holding the end of the tape," he explained as he pulled a tape measure from his back pocket. He held out the end toward her.

She took a step closer to him, her mouth unaccountably dry. What was it about him that made her feel so alive? What was it about him that seemed to invite crazy feelings and desires?

"Hold the end right here." He pointed to a stop on the end of one of the cabinets. She moved to do as he bid, and he pressed his finger against hers. "Yes, right there," he murmured, his breath warm on her face.

She breathed a sigh of relief as he moved to the

other end of the cabinet. The man had a sexual energy that positively seethed from him.

"Okay, got it," he said. "Now I need you to hold it over here." He walked to the refrigerator and waited for her to join him. "Can you reach up here?" He gestured to the bottom of the cabinet over the refrigerator.

She nodded, rose on her tiptoes reaching up. Again he placed his finger over hers, as if to assure himself she was at the right place. "Hmm, you smell good," he said.

He took a step closer to her, so close she could feel his warm breath on the back of her neck, smell the pleasant masculine scent of him.

"Thank you," she murmured breathlessly.

"I was just thinking that with your hand otherwise occupied now might be a perfect time to begin charming you."

Abby turned her head to look at him in panic. "Don't you dare," she exclaimed. "Stephanie told me you charm a woman right into seduction, and I'll tell you right now that even though the other women in this town might find you irresistible, that doesn't mean I do. You just don't have that kind of an effect on me."

"Really?" he replied with obvious amusement. He placed the tape measure on the countertop, then looked at her once again, those sinful eyes of his promising unspeakable pleasures.

"If I don't have any kind of effect on you, then why is your pulse beating so rapidly right here?" With his index finger he touched the pulse point in the hollow of her throat.

Abby swallowed hard, as if in doing so she could dispel the electric jolt his touch sent riveting through her. She knew she needed to step away from his touch, tell him in no uncertain terms that she wasn't about to become another notch on his bedpost.

And yet, there was a crazy, insane, utterly feminine pull in the opposite direction. There was no denying the fact that she was overwhelmingly attracted to Luke, and she suffered a hunger for all the things she saw in his dark, wicked eyes…uncomplicated passion and simplistic desire.

One thing was certain, she had a feeling that the last thing Luke Delaney wanted from her was any kind of real intimacy other than the physical kind. And she certainly wasn't in the position to want any kind of true intimacy with anyone. She harbored too many secrets for that.

"Why is your breathing just a little more shallow than normal?" he asked in his deep, low voice that was as seductive as a voice could be.

"I have asthma," she replied, and he laughed again, seeing through the lie. "Why would I want to get involved in any way with you," she asked lightly and stepped away from him. "From what the gossips in town say, you're rather conceited, you drink too much and you don't take anything seriously."

His eyes danced with brilliant lights of amusement. "I stopped drinking over a month ago, I'm only conceited about the things I have a right to be and I take my lovemaking very seriously."

She wasn't sure how it was possible for him to elevate her body temperature with mere words, but somehow he managed it.

"A year is a long time to be alone, Abby," he said softly, and although he didn't attempt to touch her again, the warmth of his gaze stroked her with the potency of a physical caress.

"Yes, it is," she agreed. "But that doesn't mean I'm ready to fall into bed with the first handsome man who comes along."

"Ah, so you think I'm handsome."

This time it was her turn to laugh. "You know you're handsome. But it takes more than a pretty face and sweet words to seduce me."

He leaned a hip against the counter, eyeing her with a wicked smile. "Really? Then what does it take?"

"You're just going to have to figure it out," she replied enigmatically. In truth, good sense had managed to reign over raging hormones.

She couldn't think about herself, couldn't think about her wants or needs. She had two children to consider, and it wouldn't be a good idea for her to allow Luke or any man into their life at this time.

Before he could make any kind of response, a horn bleated loudly. Abby checked her wristwatch. "That will be the school bus bringing home the kids," she said, and hurried out the kitchen door.

The bus driver waved as she stepped around the side of the house then opened the bus door. Jason and Jessica tumbled out, their faces lit with the happiness of a successful first day of school.

They raced to her, and she leaned down and

wrapped her arms around them both. "Did you have a good day?" she asked them.

"We like school," Jason exclaimed. "My teacher is really nice and I got a new best friend and we have a hamster in a cage...."

Abby laughed as the words tumbled from him. "Whoa, slow down." She turned to Jessica. "And what about you? Do you like school?" Jessica nodded, her eyes shining brightly, and Abby wondered how long it would be before she got a call from Jessica's teacher wondering why the little girl refused to speak.

She shoved this worry away. She'd deal with it when it came up. "Go change your clothes, and you can play outside." Luke's swing was a rousing success with the two children, and she knew that's where they would go.

They raced inside the house, and she followed.

"First day of school go okay?" Luke asked as she entered the kitchen.

She nodded and smiled. "It would seem so."

"I always loved school. It was the one place where I could escape from my father."

She leaned against the kitchen table and eyed him curiously. "So your father really was the meanest man on earth?"

"Definitely," he replied, and for just a moment a shadow usurped the sparkle of his eyes. "But thankfully he's gone now, I hope to his just reward."

Abby didn't know how to reply. She wanted to tell him that he was wrong, that his father couldn't be the meanest man on earth. Justin Cahill held that particular honor. Justin Cahill, who had shattered Jason and Jessica, who had stolen so much from her life and had not received his just reward, but rather had escaped the consequences of the heinous crime he'd committed.

"If you'll hold the tape measure for me again, I promise I'll behave," he said, the wicked gleam back in his eyes.

She returned his smile. "I'm not sure I can trust your promises."

"Oh, but you can. I never lie, and I never, ever break a promise."

"Then that certainly makes you different from the men I've known in my lifetime," she replied truthfully, then flushed as she realized she'd said more about her personal life than she'd intended.

They worked in silence for a few minutes, Abby holding the tape where Luke instructed her and Luke taking notes of the measurements needed to construct new cabinets.

They had just finished the last door when the kids raced in to tell Abby they were going out to the swing.

When they were gone, Luke eyed her with open speculation. "Am I to assume from your last statement that maybe your marriage wasn't exactly a happy one?"

The web of deceit Abby had spun seemed to grow more tangled, more complicated. She didn't want to tell more lies. "I'd rather not talk about it," she finally said. "And if you don't need my help in here, there are some things I need to take care of."

"I'm finished here," he replied, and she was aware

of his gaze lingering on her, filled with curiosity, as she fled the room.

Luke stared after her, more curious than ever. He could only discern from her statement that her life had been filled with men who lied and broke promises. When she'd uttered the statement that if Luke did neither, then he was different from the men in her life, she'd looked achingly vulnerable and hauntingly fragile.

He'd had the crazy impulse to take her in his arms and hold her tight. And his desire had nothing to do with anything physical, nothing to do with sex. He'd merely wanted to take away the pain that had momentarily whispered in her eyes.

Crazy, he thought as he left the kitchen by the back door.

He waved to the kids who were taking turns on the swing, then headed around to the front and began to pull down the last of the old porch. As he worked, his mind raced with thoughts of Abby.

Had her marriage been a miserable one? Was it possible her husband had lied to her, broken promises...and even worse?

Once again he thought of Jason asking him if his daddy was mean. Why would a six-year-old ask such a question unless he knew something about mean daddies?

Luke had a feeling what Abigail Graham needed more than anything in her life was some good, old-fashioned fun. She obviously had a good sense of humor. That had been evident as she'd teased him.

But how much fun could her life have been for the past year having the responsibility for raising two kids alone? And how much fun had her life contained prior to her husband's death?

He worked until dinnertime and managed to get the last of the old porch down. He'd just finished loading his tools in the back of the truck when Abby came around the side of the house.

"I was just going to come in to find you," he said. "I've got to get over to the family ranch and put in a few hours, but I'd like to come back later this evening and set the posts. That way they can set up overnight and will be ready by morning."

"That's fine with me, but I thought you worked at the Honky Tonk in the evenings."

"It's closed on Monday nights," he explained. He looked at his watch. "It's almost five now. I'll be back here about eight, if that's okay."

"Sure, that's fine with me," she agreed.

"Okay, then I'll see you about eight." He started to get in his truck, but paused. "Oh…and Abby, I've figured out what you need in your life."

"Oh, really?" She arched one of her perfect brows. "And what might that be?"

He grinned. "I'll tell you later." He slid behind the steering wheel and waved at her, then pulled away from the house.

Within minutes he was at the ranch and spent the next couple of hours repairing a fence that was threatening to topple down.

When he'd finished, he went to the main house, to

the bedroom that had been his as a child. Much of his clothing and personal belongings were still here.

When he'd moved into the Honky Tonk, he'd taken very little with him, knowing it wasn't a good idea to store anything of value in the tiny room. The ranch was close enough for him to obtain anything he might need in a short period of time.

He showered, then changed into clean clothes, his mind whirling with memories that being in this room always evoked.

When he'd been growing up, this room had served as both a retreat and a prison cell. There had been times when his father had sent him to this room, and other times when he'd run here to escape his father's rage.

He left the room and the memories behind, heading for the kitchen and a chance to grab something to eat before he returned to Abby's place.

He'd just sat down at the kitchen table with a ham sandwich when his brother Matthew walked in. "I thought I heard somebody down here," he said.

"I stopped by to shower and change clothes."

"And raid my refrigerator," Matthew added dryly.

"That, too," Luke agreed affably. "Things seem quiet around here. In a couple more weeks things will really be quiet."

"I've already started a list of things that need to be repaired in the guest cabins," Matthew said as he leaned his back against the refrigerator. He rubbed the center of his forehead with two fingers.

"Rough day?" Luke asked.

"Rough week," Matthew said as he dropped his

hand. "We've got a family in cabin four who is driving everyone crazy. I'm tired of dealing with everything. I'm really looking forward to a little downtime."

Luke looked at his oldest brother in surprise. Matthew was always efficient, in control and on top of things. Of the four, Matthew had been the one who had pushed the hardest for them to fulfill their father's will stipulations so they wouldn't lose the ranch. The idea that Matthew's eagerness to hold on to the family ranch might be waning was disconcerting.

They had to hold on to things for another few months…until the terms of the will had been met. After that, it didn't matter.

"I'm heading upstairs. Lock up when you leave," Matthew said.

Luke nodded and watched as his brother disappeared out the door. Luke finished his sandwich, then placed his dish in the dishwasher and checked his watch. Quarter to eight. Time for him to get to Abby's.

As he drove to her house, he told himself Matthew had just had a rough day. There was no way Matthew would encourage them to forget their father's will and the family ranch. Matthew was the son most like his father, and like Adam Delaney, Matthew believed the ranch was the most important thing on the face of the earth.

He pulled into Abby's place and shoved aside thoughts of his brother. Although Luke could definitely use the money that would come from the ranch if they retained control, he really didn't care if they defaulted and lost it.

He'd just raised his hand to knock on Abby's back door when it swung open. As always, at the sight of her, an electric charge shot through him. "I'm back."

"So, you are and right on time," she said.

"I just figured I'd tell you I was here so you wouldn't be frightened when you hear somebody out front. Could you turn on the front porch light for me? Then I'll just get to work," he said and started to turn away.

"Oh, no, you don't," she said, stopping him in his tracks. "What is it you've figured out I need in my life?"

He grinned. "I'm not ready to tell you yet. Maybe after I finish setting the posts."

"I'm going to hold you to it," she exclaimed.

He grinned, then turned and left. By the time he reached the front of the house the front light was shining on the space where there was now no porch.

He'd dug the holes for the posts earlier in the day, and it didn't take him too long to mix the concrete, then set the posts into the holes. In the arid heat of the night, they would set up quickly, and by morning he should be able to start constructing the new porch.

He'd finished setting the last post then walked to the back door, surprised to find Abby seated on the stoop and gazing at the stars.

"Stargazing?" He sat next to her on the stoop and instantly caught a whiff of her evocative perfume.

"Yes. I can't seem to get enough of the stars out here. They all look so much closer, so much bigger and brighter."

"That's because they are tools the cowboys use."

She eyed him ruefully. "Let me guess. Cowboys use the stars to seduce young women."

He laughed. "You brought it up this time, I didn't. I was going to say that the cowboys used to use the stars for direction."

"I'm impressed," she said with a teasing tone. "You can talk about things other than charming women."

He smiled. "Where are the munchkins?"

"In bed. I tucked them in about an hour ago. Apparently the first day of school was rather exhausting. Neither of them gave me a bedtime argument."

"I wouldn't give you a bedtime argument, either," he said, unable to help himself.

"You're terrible," she replied, and he knew the color of her cheeks had deepened to a bewitching pink.

"That's not true," he countered. "I've been told I'm very good."

She laughed and shook her head, causing her hair to dance like a silken waterfall around her slender shoulders. Luke liked the sound of her laughter and guessed that she probably hadn't had much laughter in her life the past year.

"Okay, I said I'd tell you what I think you need in your life," he said.

"And what might that be?" she asked cautiously.

"Just some good, old-fashioned fun."

Her gaze held his for a long moment, and in the depths of her beautiful, soft green eyes he saw he had touched a vulnerable area.

He fought the impulse to throw his arm over her

shoulder, pull her tight against his side. He was afraid he might spook her by moving too fast.

"I get the feeling that there hasn't been much fun in your life for the past year," he finally said.

"That's true," she agreed softly, her eyes holding a wistful yearning.

"You should come down to the Honky Tonk some night," he said.

"To watch you perform?" she asked.

"Nah. You need to come in and kick up your heels, do a little boot-scoot boogie."

She laughed. "I don't know how to do a boot-scoot boogie. In fact, I can't remember the last time I danced."

"You're kidding. Your husband didn't take you out dancing?"

She broke eye contact with him and once again gazed at the star-studded skies. "No, he never took me dancing."

Luke stared at her in amazement. If he had a wife who looked like her, he'd take her dancing every chance he got just for the opportunity of holding her close and swaying in rhythm to whatever music played. Her husband must have been a fool.

Luke wasn't a fool. Before he could stop himself, he stood, grabbed her hand and pulled her off the stoop and into his arms in a traditional dance position. "Ever danced with a cowboy carpenter beneath a star-lit sky?"

"Never," she replied, her voice slightly husky.

"Then you're about to experience one of life's little

joys.'' And with these words, he whirled her around, tightening his grip on her waist as they spun.

She held herself rigid and unyielding for a few moments, but when he didn't try to pull her tightly against him, he felt her relaxing by degrees.

As he hummed a familiar ballad, she continued to become more fluid, stepping and swaying with him as a night breeze danced in her hair and the moonlight kissed her features. And as he felt the rigidity leaving her, he pulled her closer...closer...and closer still.

Finally she was where he wanted her, so close her thighs pressed against his and her breasts snuggled against his chest. Her warm breath fanned his collarbone, producing a heat inside him that had nothing to do with the warmth of the night air that surrounded them.

Suddenly they weren't dancing anymore. They stood in the embrace, and when she turned her face to look at him, the tune he'd been humming died on his lips.

Just a whisper of invitation lit her eyes as her mouth parted slightly. It was all the invitation Luke needed. He captured her mouth with his, stealing a kiss that was freely given.

Her instantaneous response surprised and enflamed him. He'd intended for the kiss to be a light, sweet gesture, but her mouth was too hot, too hungry, and stirred a wild hunger inside him.

He dipped his tongue into her mouth, at the same time pressing his hand into the small of her back. Her tongue met his, deepening the kiss to explosive heights.

She moaned deep in the back of her throat and lifted her arms, wrapping them around his neck as their bodies pressed more tightly against each other.

A scream shattered the moment, a scream of such childish terror, it raised the hairs on the nape of Luke's neck. "What the hell?" he exclaimed as a new source of adrenaline shot through him.

Abby whirled out of his arms and raced up the steps to the back door. "It's Jason," she said and disappeared into the house.

The scream came again, high-pitched and frantic. Luke hurried into the house and down the hallway to the little boy's room.

He stepped into the doorway to see Abby trying to control a flailing, fighting Jason. It was obvious the little boy was still asleep, but that didn't stop his churning arms and legs. As Luke stood hesitantly, he saw one of Jason's elbows crash into Abby's chin. He took a step forward, intent on helping her, but she stopped him.

"Please...just go," she said, her eyes begging him to comply. Still he hesitated, wanting to help. "For God's sake, Luke. Leave," she said more forcefully. "We'll talk tomorrow."

As she focused her attention on the flailing child, Luke hesitated another moment, then complied with her wishes. He left the bedroom and went down the hallway toward the door. The childish screams had stopped, but he could hear Jason sobbing. They were deep, rending sobs that tore at Luke. And beneath the sobs he could hear Abby's soft, soothing voice.

Luke stepped onto the back stoop and drew a deep,

unsteady breath, allowing the momentary burst of adrenaline to slide away. The transformation from desire to panic had been abrupt, and the result was confusion.

He suspected he knew the source of Abby's black eye and the bruise on her arm. In trying to soothe Jason, she apparently became a battle-scarred warrior.

He got into his truck, his thoughts whirling. It was obvious Jason had been suffering a horrendous nightmare. What could a little boy possibly dream about that would cause such obvious terror?

A little boy who had nightmares, a little girl who didn't talk and a woman whose kiss had shot wildfire through his veins. Luke had a feeling if he didn't take care, he'd be in way over his head with this woman and her children.

Chapter 6

Sleep was a long time coming for Abby after she finally got Jason settled into a peaceful sleep. She undressed and got ready for bed, but her thoughts whirled chaotically.

She'd hoped that in settling here, in building a home and establishing some semblance of normalcy, Jason's nightmares would finally stop.

She knew they'd only been here a little over a week, and she was probably expecting way too much, way too soon. But she couldn't help the deep depression the little boy's latest nightmare had instilled in her.

How long would he suffer the remnants of that night? Somehow she had to figure out a way to heal the two children who had been left in her care by the sister she'd loved and lost.

Sliding between the sheets, she knew she needed to seek professional help for the kids. They had been seeing a therapist before they'd left Kansas City, and on their last visit, the therapist had told Abby she thought a physical move from the city would do as much to heal the kids as anything.

But Jessica was still not talking, and Jason was still having horrendous nightmares. No healing appeared to be taking place.

She had a feeling finding a good therapist who specialized in traumatized children would be impossible in the small town of Inferno. She'd need to go to Tucson or another big city to find them help.

Too tired to think about it anymore, she closed her eyes, and instantly a vision of Luke filled her mind. Luke, with the moonlight stroking his bold, handsome features. Luke, his lips curved in a smile as he hummed and twirled her around in his arms.

For one sweet moment, the cares of the world had fallen from her shoulders and she'd felt young and desirable and carefree. And then there was the kiss. The kiss.

She pushed the sheet aside. Heat swirled through her as she remembered the hunger, the fire, the utter desire that she'd not only tasted in his kiss, but had felt inside herself as she'd responded to him.

Abby was no virgin—she'd been engaged to be married before the crime that had destroyed her world. But none of Ken's kisses, none of his caresses had ever stirred her like Luke's kiss had done.

When he'd stood in Jason's doorway and seen her struggling with the frantic little boy, she'd seen his desire to help in his eyes, and that had been nearly as powerful as his kiss in managing to creep in beneath her defenses.

She closed her eyes, too tired to think about any of it tonight. Tomorrow she would get on the phone and try to find a therapist for the kids. Tomorrow she would figure out exactly how much she was going to tell Luke about Jason's nightmares. She was going to have to decide if it was safe to divulge any of her secrets to Luke Delaney.

Morning brought few answers. She had just put the kids on the school bus when Luke's familiar pickup approached.

She stood in the front yard as he pulled up and got out of the truck, looking as handsome, as strong and masculine as she'd ever seen him. "Hi," she greeted him as he strode toward her.

"Hi, yourself," he returned easily. "You look tired."

"I am," she admitted. "It was kind of a long night."

He stepped next to her, the gray of his eyes soft and his smile gentle. "I wanted to help but didn't know how." He threw an arm around her shoulder. "You got the coffee on?"

She nodded, fighting the impulse to lean into him, to spill the events that had shaped her life for the past year, to share the pain that radiated inside her and she feared would always exist inside her.

Together they went into the house and to the kitchen, where Luke gestured her into a chair at the table while he took it upon himself to pour them some coffee.

"I guess I owe you some sort of an explanation," she said when he was seated at the table next to her.

"You don't owe me anything," he countered with the same gentleness of tone, the gentleness that reached inside her and stroked a tiny piece of her pain. "It's obvious from what I saw last night that your son suffers terrible nightmares or night terrors."

"He's not my son." Horror swept through her as she realized she'd spoken the words aloud.

Luke's eyes widened. "Excuse me? But they call you Mom and you introduced them as your kids."

Abby wrapped her hands around her coffee cup, recognizing that this was the moment she had to decide if she could trust Luke or not. She quickly decided she would trust him with some of the truth. "Jason isn't my son, and Jessica isn't my daughter. They are my nephew and niece."

"Your sister's kids?"

Abby nodded. "I took custody of them when their mother was murdered."

Again Luke's eyes widened. "Murdered?"

Emotion rose inside Abby, a wave she felt helpless to fight against. She nodded again, then took a sip of coffee in an attempt to steady herself. "In order for you to understand, I guess I need to start at the beginning." She frowned, wondering if she knew what had been the beginning.

"My sister, Loretta, was married to a man named Justin Cahill. Neither my parents nor I particularly liked Justin. He was a braggart and never held down a job. He was verbally abusive to her and the kids.

But Loretta seemed to love him so we all tried our best to make him part of our family.''

She drew a deep breath and stared into her coffee mug. ''A month before her murder, I realized Justin was being more than verbally abusive to her, and I convinced her the best thing to do was divorce him. I helped her find a little apartment, and she and the kids moved into it. Three weeks later Justin came to the apartment and beat her to death. Jessica and Jason were in the apartment when it happened.''

''Oh, God, I'm so sorry.'' His hand instantly sought hers in a warm grip of comfort. ''And that's why Jason has nightmares.'' It was more a statement than a question.

''Actually, what he's doing is replaying that night in his dreams. And, according to the therapist Jason was seeing before we moved, in his sleep he tries to fight with his father to save his mother's life.''

''That poor kid,'' Luke said, and she heard the wealth of sympathy in his voice as his hand tightened around hers. ''Jessica stopped talking at the same time?''

''Yes. That night the police removed the kids from the apartment and brought them to me. Jessica told me about how her daddy had hurt her mommy, and that's the last time Jessica said anything to anyone except Jason.''

She cleared her throat. ''Anyway, so now you know the explanation for Jason's nightmares.'' But there was a wealth of information she hadn't given him, like the small fact that she didn't have legal authority to have the children in her custody and that they were on the run from Justin…and possibly the law.

"So why the story of you being a widow? Are you or were you married?"

"No." Abby pulled her hand from his and once again wrapped both hands around her coffee mug. "I'm not, nor have I ever been married. I made up that story so we wouldn't have to explain to people what had happened. I thought it would make things easier on the children. It was Jason's idea to call me Mom. He said I would be his mom on earth, but we always talk about their mother in heaven." Her voice cracked on the last sentence, and she drew a deep breath to steady herself.

He nodded, his eyes curiously opaque. "That it makes things easier on the children is the best reason to tell a lie. What about their father? Where is he?"

"Nobody knows. Apparently he's disappeared off the face of the earth, and that's just fine with me." But Abby knew Justin was looking for them, hunting them down like prey. And she hoped he never, ever found them.

"When you told me you'd had a rough year, you weren't kidding. How are you holding up beneath all this?"

She looked away from him, unable to see the compassion in his eyes and not fall apart. "My sister was my best friend. It was me who encouraged her to leave Justin in the first place." She fought against a wave of killing guilt. "But I'm all right. I'm strong."

She drew a breath and squared her shoulders. "I have to be for the kids. They're the ones I worry about.

They have to live not only with the memory of that terrible night, but also with the knowledge that their father is a bad man.''

Luke leaned back in his chair. "Kids are fairly resilient, and I'm a perfect example that kids can grow up and eventually deal with the fact that their father is a bad man.''

"But your father didn't kill your mother," she replied.

"That's true," he agreed easily. "But there were times I thought sure he was going to kill one of my brothers, or my sister, or me.''

"He was really that mean?" she asked even though she could tell by his somber expression and the heavy tone of voice that he wasn't exaggerating.

"I thought he was the devil.''

"How did you survive?''

He shrugged. "We just did." This time it was his turn to take a sip of his coffee before continuing. "Actually, the four of us all had our own way of coping with Father. Matthew was the good son who never broke the rules and worked from sunup to sundown with the single goal of pleasing the old man. Mark became invisible, never talking, trying to blend into the woodwork so he wouldn't do anything to upset the old man.''

He took another sip of his coffee and grinned. "Johnna, on the other hand, did just the opposite. She met my father with rebellion and rage and kept him stirred up most of the time.''

"And what about you?" Abby asked.

"Me? I learned how to sing. It was the one thing I

did that pleased the old man. My dad used to play George Reeves records when we were growing up. By the time I was six I knew all the words to all the songs. One day my dad heard me singing in my room, and he called me down to his study and demanded I sing for him.''

He drew a deep breath, and Abby saw the pain of memories cross his features. She reached for his hand, as he had done to her earlier. His hand was cool, as if the force of these memories had stolen all his body heat.

''I went down to the study, knowing that if he didn't like my singing he'd smack me or take off his belt and whack me. I was so scared that while I sang for him, I wet my pants.''

''Oh, Luke.'' All thoughts of Abby's problems and worries fell aside as she grieved for the little boy who had sung for a monster and been so afraid he'd wet his pants.

Emotion swam in the air, inside her, a depth of emotion for him and for the children she now claimed as her own.

She released his hand only long enough to leave her chair, and as she stood, he did, as well. Together they met in an embrace. His arms wrapped around her, and she allowed herself to accept the comfort, the warmth and the strength she found there.

Leaning her head against his broad chest, she could hear the pounding of his heart. ''Your kids will be okay, Abby,'' he said softly. ''They're lucky to have you. With your love and support they're going to be just fine.''

She'd hungered to hear those words from anyone, and for a moment her fears about the kids were soothed. She lifted her head from his chest and looked at him. She'd meant to thank him, to say how much his words meant to her, but the moment she saw the fire in his eyes, anything she might have meant to say left her mind.

His lips crashed down on hers and instantly Abby knew she was going to make love with him. Not tomorrow. Not next week. Today, at this moment, while they had the house to themselves and their depth of emotion had been transformed into lust.

She wanted to be held, heartbeat to heartbeat, skin against skin. She needed to lose herself in the flames that lit his eyes and scorched her lips as his kiss sent electric currents racing through her.

Luke didn't have to be the right man in her life to be the right man at this moment. She gave herself to him, pressing against him with need, meeting his tongue with her own, stoking the flames of desire between them until they were totally out of control.

Making love to Abby had been the last thing in Luke's mind when he'd reached out to her. He'd been shocked by the information she'd shared with him, and equally shocked by how candid he'd been with her about his past with his father.

But holding her, feeling her soft curves against him as her sweet scent filled his head, desire had unexpectedly awakened.

When her lips met his with the same intense fever coupled with a yielding surrender, he was lost...lost despite the fact he knew they were moving too quickly and on the wave of heightened emotions.

He finally pulled his mouth from hers. He stared at her, and in her eyes he saw a hunger that matched his own. "Abby." He knew one of them needed to take control of the situation before it spun crazily out of control.

"Shh." She pressed two fingers to his lips then took his hand in hers and led him out of the kitchen. "Don't stop this, Luke. It's what you want, and for right now it's what I want."

As she pulled him down the hallway toward her bedroom, Luke's heart boomed rapidly. He'd wanted her from the first minute he'd laid eyes on her, and that desire had grown with each and every moment he'd spent in her company.

The morning sunlight streamed into her bedroom window, and he noticed that her room had been transformed since last time he'd peeked into it. The bed was neatly made with a bedspread that was a splash of yellow sunflowers.

Where before there had been a stack of boxes in the corner, there were now only two waiting to be unpacked.

He scarcely had time to take all this in before his attention returned to Abby, who stood next to the bed. As he watched her, she pulled her T-shirt over her head.

His breath caught in his chest at the sight of her. Clad in her jeans and a wispy, pale pink bra, she appeared fragile and more vulnerable than before. But the glow in her eyes as she unfastened her jeans and slid them down her slender legs was anything but vulnerable.

He drank in the sight of her in the few seconds he had before she pulled down the spread and disappeared beneath the sheets on the bed.

"Do you always keep your women waiting?"

Her husky voice broke his inertia, and he ripped his T-shirt over his head and threw it on the floor. He felt as if his fingers had all turned to thumbs as he worked the buttons on his fly. Before he allowed his jeans to fall on the floor, he took out his wallet, opened it and withdrew a foil package.

When he was naked, he hesitated at the edge of the bed. He knew they had stirred up powerful emotions as they'd talked of their pasts, and he wanted to give her a chance to change her mind, didn't want to in any way be accused of taking advantage of her vulnerability.

"Luke, I promise no recriminations, no expectations."

Her words removed the last barrier between Luke and his desire for her. He placed the foil package on the nightstand, then slid beneath the sheets and reached out to her.

She came willingly to meet him, her body pressing against his as their lips sought each other in frenzied need. Luke had thought he'd spent the last week quietly seducing her, but he realized she'd been doing some seducing of her own. She'd stoked in him a fire of desire he'd never felt before.

When he finally broke the kiss, he moved his lips down her jawline into the hollow of her throat. She wrapped her arms around his neck, pulling him more tightly against her.

His hands crept up to cup her breasts. Despite the silky material of her bra, he could feel her taut nipples beneath his fingertips. He raked his thumb across the tips and reveled at the sweet moan that escaped her.

It took only moments for him to grow frustrated by the material that kept their bodies separate. With a groan, he reached behind her and unfastened her bra, then swept his hands downward to steal away her panties.

She aided him in his efforts, shrugging the bra from her shoulders and raising her hips, then kicking off the lacy panties.

He knew he wouldn't be able to last too long, that the moment he entered her all control would be lost. And before that happened, he wanted to make love to her, to taste her sweet skin, to touch her in ways that made her wild with wanting him.

And that's exactly what he did. With the golden shine of sunlight slanting into the window, he threw back the sheets and made love to her.

He loved the scent of her, the taste of her skin and the way she responded to each touch, every caress. She was an active lover, matching him touch for touch, kiss for kiss, caress for caress.

Although he would have loved to make love to her throughout the morning hours, all too quickly he felt himself reaching the point of no return.

"Luke," she said, her voice taut with need. "Please...I want you."

That's all he needed to hear. He picked up the foil

package, surprised when she took it from him. Her eyes glittered with anticipation as she tore open the foil and removed the protective sheath.

Her fingers were hot and radiated urgency as she rolled the condom onto his throbbing member. Immediately, he got on top of her and she parted her legs to welcome him. With one smooth motion he entered her, sliding into her tight warmth as a groan of intense pleasure escaped him.

Her fingers dug into his back as he remained motionless, overwhelmed by sensation and momentarily afraid to move. He drew several deep breaths, fighting for control, then slowly, almost imperceptibly began to move his hips against hers in the age-old rhythm of need.

He meant it to be slow and easy, building to a shattering conclusion. But it was impossible to go slow and easy. The sensations that rippled through him demanded faster…frenzied. And Abby demanded it, as well, setting the pace with hip thrusts that took him higher and higher.

It wasn't until she stiffened and cried out in splendor that he allowed himself the final release. Wave after wave of pleasure swept over him until he was gasping and spent.

He rolled to her side, pulled her against him and waited for their breathing to return to normal. She curled against him, and he was vaguely aware of how well their bodies fit together. With her head on his shoulder, they fit together like puzzle pieces.

He stroked a hand through her hair, marveling that

it was, indeed, just as soft and silky as he'd imagined. "You okay?" he asked softly.

"At the moment I'm better than okay. I feel simply marvelous."

"That's because I'm a marvelous lover," he teased. "Hadn't I mentioned that before?"

She laughed. "I believe you might have mentioned it before. I guess I can tell Stephanie that your legendary charm overwhelmed me," she said lightly.

He grinned. "I think I was the one that was overwhelmed by your considerable charm. Besides, one single occurrence does not a success make," he countered.

For a long moment they remained quiet, neither seemingly eager to break their embrace. "I'm sorry about your father being so mean," she finally said.

He leaned on one elbow and looked at her. The sunlight painted her face in golden tones, making her eyes appear a striking green. "And I'm sorry about your sister." He gazed at her curiously. "What about your parents? Were they good ones?"

Her lips curved into a smile that shot a new wave of desire through him. "They were the best. They were kind and loving and wonderfully supportive." A tiny frown creased the center of her forehead. "What about your mother? You've never mentioned her."

"She died giving birth to Johnna. I was only a year old at the time, so I never really knew her."

She reached up and placed her palm against his cheek. "I wish you would have had the kind of parents I had."

"Are they still around?"

A dark shadow stole the sparkle of her eyes. "No. They died four years ago in a car accident. I'm just grateful they weren't around to know about Loretta. I think her death would have killed them." The shadow disappeared. "And now we'd better get out of this bed."

In one fluid movement, she left his arms and rolled out of bed. He sat up and watched as she grabbed her bra and panties then disappeared into the adjoining bathroom.

He remained in the bed as he heard the sound of a shower starting, deciding that when she finished, he'd jump in for a quick cleanup.

His body still retained her fragrance, a scent that would be distracting as he worked the remainder of the afternoon. Even now, as he breathed deeply, he felt a renewed stir of desire for her.

He frowned, not particularly pleased to find himself wanting her again so quickly, so strongly. It also bothered him that he had confided so much of his past to her. He'd never, ever told anyone about singing for his father and wetting his pants. Why on earth had he told her of that particular little embarrassing incident?

He was still ruminating over this when she entered the bedroom clad in a bathrobe. "Abby...about what just happened..." he began, feeling the need to somehow insert a little distance between them.

She held up her hand to silence him. "I told you, Luke. No recriminations and no expectations. What happened, happened. It's over, it's done."

She sat on the edge of the bed and gazed at him somberly. "When Loretta was murdered, I was engaged to a man who professed to love children and value family above all else. When he realized I was taking on two scarred, frightened children, I expected him to be by my side, but he ran for the hills. When my sister left her husband, I thought that finally she was going to get a chance to live a happy, normal life, but I was wrong.''

She got up from the edge of the bed and grabbed her jeans and her T-shirt. ''I've learned the hard way to expect nothing from life or from people. I take it one day at a time.'' She offered him a strained smile. ''Don't worry, Luke. As far as I'm concerned, we can forget this happened at all. The bathroom is all yours. I'll finish dressing in one of the kids' rooms.'' With these words she left the bedroom.

Luke stared after her, oddly disturbed by her words, and bothered that her words had disturbed him.

Chapter 7

Abby was almost grateful the next morning when Luke called her and said he wouldn't be able to work at her place that day.

She needed the day without his magnetic presence to get the ground firmly beneath her feet and deal with the embarrassment the events of the day before had created in her.

She had probably been the easiest seduction the man had ever successfully completed. She'd practically thrown herself at him, insisting that he make love to her. Her cheeks burned at the memory of how forward she'd been and how glorious being in his arms had felt.

She'd known from the moment she'd met Luke, when he'd teased her with those sooty eyes of his, that he would be a magnificent lover, and she hadn't been wrong.

He'd been gentle yet masterful, sweeping her into the heights of delight with hungry kisses and hot caresses. When his dark eyes had gazed at her, he'd made her feel more beautiful and more desirable than anyone had ever made her feel.

With utter mastery and confidence, he'd known just where to touch, just how to kiss to produce a fiery hunger for him inside her.

She spent the entire day trying to forget the power of his kisses, the warm comfort of his arms, the utter splendor of his naked body against hers.

He called the next morning and told her once again that he had other business that wouldn't allow him to get to her place that day. She wondered if perhaps he was trying to avoid her, and that only increased her embarrassment over the intimacy that had occurred between them.

It was early Thursday morning, and she was standing at the edge of the road with the children waiting for the school bus, when she saw Luke's familiar black pickup heading in their direction.

She couldn't help the small lurch of her heart as he parked the truck and stepped out. He was so darned sexy in his tight, worn jeans and the white T-shirt that pulled provocatively across the width of his chest.

His thick, dark hair gleamed in the sun and despite herself her gaze swept across his chest to his bulging biceps, and she remembered how good it had felt to lay in his strong arms.

He waved but didn't approach. Instead he walked to the back of the truck and unloaded several pieces of lumber.

"What's he doing now?" Jason asked, his dark eyes focused on Luke.

"He's going to finish building us a nice, new porch," Abby explained.

Jason eyed her somberly, a tiny frown on his forehead. "When I'm in school, is he nice to you?"

Abby saw the worry in his eyes and leaned down to draw his little body closer to hers. "He's very nice." Jessica stepped closer, as if she, too, momentarily needed the warmth of Abby's arms around her.

"There are good men and there are bad men," she said to them. "Luke is a good man. He's making our house nice, and he's nice to me. He makes me smile."

"If he's mean to you, I'll kick him," Jason exclaimed with a burst of little-boy bravado.

"You know that kicking somebody is unacceptable," Abby chided softly. "Besides, Luke would never do anything to hurt me. He's a nice man."

At that moment the school bus lumbered into view. She gave each child a hug. "Now, you have a great day at school and I'll see you later this afternoon. We're safe here, and nobody is going to hurt me or either of you."

She saw them safely on the bus, then as the big yellow vehicle pulled away, she waved to them until they were out of sight.

Jason's concern for her safety was not surprising, but it was heartbreaking nevertheless. A six-year-old boy should never have to worry about the physical safety of an adult.

Surely they were all safe. It had been two months since the debacle of a trial, two months in which she'd heard no word from Justin Cahill, the man who'd murdered her sister and who was the father of the children.

As she turned to walk toward the house, she steeled herself for interacting with the man she'd made love to three days before.

"Morning," he said as he opened his toolbox and began to lay out what he'd need to begin work. "I see you got the munchkins off okay."

She nodded, aware of the uncomfortable tension that thickened the air between them. "Can I get you anything before you get started? A cup of coffee or something?"

"No, I'm fine," he replied briskly. "This is going to take a lot of work so I'd better get right to it."

She hadn't realized how much she'd enjoyed his easy company or his lighthearted banter until now with its conspicuous absence. "Okay, just let me know if you need anything," she replied then went into the house.

It's better this way, she told herself as she went into Jason's room to begin the morning task of making beds. A business relationship was all she'd ever wanted from Luke Delaney to begin with, and things had just careened out of control the afternoon they'd made love.

It was obvious from his distance that he was done with her, had accomplished his mission, and that was fine with her. He'd given her an afternoon of sweet warmth, of intense pleasure, and all she expected from him now was carpentry work.

She spent the morning on chores, making beds and picking up clutter the children had left around the house. She consciously tried to stay away from the front of the house where she could hear the sounds of a man at work. She fought the desire to stand at the front window and watch him work, to hide behind the curtains and drink her fill of him.

However, at noon, with her stomach growling for lunch, she left the house by the back door and walked around front to see if Luke wanted to join her for lunch.

He was nowhere in sight, and his truck was gone. Apparently he wasn't interested in eating lunch with her. She fixed herself a sandwich, knowing he'd be back.

She ate the sandwich then decided to unpack the last two boxes that were in her bedroom. She'd put off unpacking them because she knew the boxes contained mostly items that had belonged to Loretta.

A half an hour later she sat on the floor of her bedroom, surrounded by an array of items that held no real monetary value but things she'd thought the children might want someday.

Each item Abby pulled out brought with it a pang of grief and yet a wealth of happy memories. There were several photographs of Abby and Loretta together as children and a couple of them as teenagers. There was a book Loretta had loved to read aloud to the younger Abby. Knickknacks, a stuffed bunny missing its nose—the box was filled with treasures. There was even a guitar with broken strings.

"Abby?"

She jumped at the sound of Luke's deep voice and looked up to see him standing hesitantly in the bedroom doorway. "Sorry, I knocked but apparently you didn't hear me." He stepped into the room, curiosity lighting his eyes. "Hey, where did you get the guitar?" He stepped closer as she held it out to him.

"It was my sister's," she explained as he took it from her and examined it. "Loretta was always looking for ways to expand her horizons, better herself and her education." She gestured to a stack of cassette tapes nearby. "She learned French in ten easy sessions, painted an oil painting with videotape instructions. At one time or another she took guitar lessons, ballet classes and played the drums."

"Sounds like a fun person," Luke said softly.

Abby offered him a full smile. "She was the best. She had a lust for living that was enviable. I thought maybe Jason or Jessica might decide to play the guitar so I packed it along with this other stuff to bring with us."

"They won't be able to play it without strings." He handed the guitar to her, the expression in his eyes inscrutable. "George Marley at the general store always orders strings for me. I could pick some up and string it for you."

"Thanks, I'd appreciate it." She got up off the floor, suddenly far too aware of the two of them alone in her bedroom, the place of their recent indiscretion. "Were you looking for me for something?" she asked, then felt the heat of a blush sweep over her cheeks as his gaze flickered to the bed, then quickly back to her.

"I could use your help outside for a few minutes. I need another hand, that is if you don't mind helping."

"Not at all." She hated the stiff formality between

them, the uncomfortable tension that filled the air, but was too embarrassed to broach the subject in order to break the ice.

She followed him outside, and with him showing her what to do, helped by balancing two two-by-eights in place so he could nail the support beams.

"Sorry I couldn't make it the last couple of days," he said as he grabbed a hammer. He hammered in a nail. "We had a fence go completely down at the ranch, and it required immediate attention."

"You don't have to apologize," she replied. "Besides, it really worked out well because yesterday I kept the kids out of school and drove into Tucson for a counseling appointment."

"How did it go?"

She shot him a quick smile. "I don't know how much help one session offered the kids, but it certainly helped me just knowing we've started getting them some help."

He hammered in another nail, then looked at her. "I told you before, they're lucky to have you on their side."

"It's the least I can do for Loretta. She and I were so close, and she was my strength when our parents died. I'm just giving back to her kids all the love she gave to me when she was alive."

He nodded and worked for a few minutes in silence, a frown creasing his forehead. She could smell him, the scent that had by now become familiar. It was the scent of maleness and bright sunshine and a faint wisp of woodsy cologne.

Instantly it brought to mind the sensual pleasure of

their morning spent in her bed. Not only had his fragrance wrapped around her, but his body had, as well, warming her from the outside in.

"Do the kids like to ride?"

"Ride?" She stared at him blankly as she consciously worked to dispel the images of making love to him.

"Horses?"

"I don't think either of them have ever been on a horse," Abby replied.

"What about you? You like to ride?" For the first time since he'd arrived, she was grateful to feel the tension between them ebbing somewhat.

"I used to love to ride, but I haven't since I was a kid."

"If you want, I could set it up so you and the kids could take a trail ride over at the ranch some time. I've never met a kid who didn't want to ride a horse."

"Thanks." She smiled at him warmly. "That would really be nice."

"It's no big deal. We've got plenty of horses that are real sweet-tempered for kids." He hammered another nail. "Okay, you can let go. I can handle it from here."

She nodded and turned to hurry into the house, away from him. She knew that making love to him three days earlier had been a mistake. What she couldn't understand was why on earth she was thinking of how nice it would be to repeat the error of her ways.

The moment Luke had seen Abby's smile, he'd wondered why he had stayed away from her for the past couple of days.

When he'd left after making love to her, he'd felt off balance, out of sorts. Although she had said all the words about no expectations he'd wanted to hear after he'd made love to her, something had bothered him.

He'd figured it out that evening as he'd nursed a soft drink at the Honky Tonk. It wasn't the lovemaking that had bothered him. That had been magnificent. It had been the emotional intimacy they'd shared just prior to falling into bed that had disturbed him.

Never before had he given quite so much of himself to a woman. Telling her about the first time he'd sung for his father, sharing with her the enormous emotional turmoil the incident had created, had shocked him and left him feeling oddly vulnerable.

Luke didn't like feeling vulnerable. He'd been vulnerable as a kid and had vowed he'd never feel that way again.

And so he'd distanced himself, taking the last couple of days to find his balance once again. He'd put in his hours at the ranch for the week and had finished the rocking chair for Rita Sue Ellenbee to sell on consignment in her craft store. He had kept himself busy and tried to keep his mind off Abigail Graham.

He straightened and swiped a hand across his brow as the school bus pulled up and Jason and Jessica got off. Jessica raced directly into the house, but Jason walked over to Luke.

He peered into Luke's toolbox with interest. ''What's that?'' he asked, pointing to a blue-handled Sheetrock knife.

"It's for cutting Sheetrock," Luke explained.

Jason tilted his head to one side and moved closer to Luke, bringing with him that special scent of boyhood. It was the smell of sweaty hair and sunshine, an earthiness that wasn't unpleasant. "What's Sheetrock?" he asked.

Luke thought of what Abby had shared with him about the horror the kids had been through, and despite his reluctance, he felt a certain kinship with the little boy.

Luke hadn't had an Abby to take control and make things right. He hadn't had an Abby to provide stability and love in his childhood. Admiration for the woman who had taken in the two kids fluttered through him.

"Sheetrock is the stuff that makes the walls in a house," he said to Jason.

"Why would you want to cut the walls?" Jason asked.

"Sometimes you get a hole in a wall accidentally and you use the knife to cut a new piece to fit into the hole," Luke said.

Jason eyed him soberly. "My mom says you're a good man, that you wouldn't ever hurt her."

Compassion swept through Luke. "I always try not to hurt anyone," he replied. He crouched so he was eye to eye with the boy. "And I promise you I'll never, ever hurt your mom."

Jason held his gaze for a long moment, then nodded as if satisfied. "But, if you ever do hurt her, I'm gonna kick you really hard."

"There you are," Abby said as she rounded the side

of the house. "I was wondering where you disappeared to. Come on inside, honey. You don't need to
be bothering Luke."

"He's not bothering me," Luke replied as he
straightened. "We were just talking about tools and
man kind of things."

Jason's little chest puffed out. "Yeah, man things,"
he agreed.

"Well, I just thought a certain little man might want
some chocolate chip cookies and milk with his sister,"
Abby said. Jason frowned, obviously torn between the
allure of cookies and the appeal of watching Luke
work.

"I know if I had the chance to eat cookies, I'd jump
on it," Luke said.

"You could come in and eat a cookie with us,"
Jason said.

Luke could tell that Abby was as surprised by the
boy's invitation as he was. Until this afternoon, Jason
had remained suspicious, downright wary of Luke.

Luke set down his hammer. "I suppose I could
choke down a cookie or two," he agreed. He was only
agreeing because he could use a little break, he told
himself. The sun was hotter than a firecracker, and a
few minutes of coolness in the house would revive his
flagging energy.

Minutes later the four of them sat at the kitchen
table, milk in front of each and a platter of cookies in
the center of the table.

"Robert Goodman has a pet lizard," Jason said.
"He brung it to school today so we could all see it."

"He brought it to school," Abby corrected.

"That's what I said," Jason replied impatiently.

Luke grinned and listened as Jason extolled the virtues of owning such a creature. He tried not to notice how pretty Abby looked in a forest green T-shirt that did amazing things to her eyes.

He wanted her again. Sitting across from her at the table, seeing her laughing and interacting with the kids, the hint of a milk mustache above her upper lip, desire slammed into him. And just as suddenly, he couldn't remember why he thought he needed distance from her in the first place.

"I think we should get a pet lizard," Jason said, drawing Luke's attention to the conversation.

"Sorry, there is positively, absolutely no way I'm having a lizard in this house," Abby exclaimed. "Personally, I think they're a little creepy."

"Then how about a dog?" Jason replied and Luke could tell by the expression on the boy's face that this had been the ultimate goal to begin with.

"A dog?" Abby looked at Jason, then at Jessica, who nodded eagerly, her eyes shining with excitement.

"I think they're ganging up on you," Luke observed with a grin, then shoved back his chair. "And this sounds like a family kind of decision, so I'll just scoot outside and get back to work."

Luke left the house to the sound of Jason promising all the things boys for an eternity had promised about taking care of a dog.

He'd wanted a dog when he'd been young, but he'd been afraid to get one, afraid that his father would hurt the pet to punish him.

He shoved the thought out of his mind and returned

to the work at hand. It was dusk when he finished for the day and packed up his tools. The porch was slowly taking shape but would require at least two or three more full days to complete. Normally he hired a high school kid to help him on the bigger jobs like decks, but with school in session, Luke had decided to do this job alone.

Besides, if he'd had a high school kid working with him he wouldn't have had the opportunity to make love to Abby. If he had a high school kid working with him, he'd probably never get an opportunity to make love to her again.

With his tools packed away, he walked to the back of the house and knocked on the door.

She stepped onto the stoop, the fading sunlight kissing her features with a golden hue. "Knocking off for the day?"

He nodded and grinned. "But I couldn't leave without knowing who won the battle."

"The battle?" She looked at him, those green eyes of hers lit with curiosity.

Again he was struck by a swelling wave of desire for her as he remembered how her green eyes had shimmered beneath half-closed lids as he'd made love to her. He jammed his hands in his pockets to stymie his desire to grab her and pull her close, capture her kissable lips with his.

"The dog battle," he replied, trying to focus on the conversation and not on his pulsing, pounding, crazy need.

She smiled. "The verdict is still out where the dog is concerned."

"Dogs are good for kids," he replied. He could vividly remember the taste of her lips...hot, sweet honey that had flowed through his veins as his mouth had possessed hers over and over again.

He took a step away from her, consciously willing his mind to stop its thoughts. "If you decide you want to get them a dog, let me know. There are a couple of breeders in the area, some that are reputable and some you should stay away from."

"Thanks, Luke. For everything." For a brief moment he saw in her eyes that she wasn't just talking about his carpentry work, that she, too, was remembering the morning they'd spent in one another's arms.

He nodded and took another step backward. "I'll see you in the morning." He turned to leave, then whirled to face her. "How about on Saturday I come and pick up you and the kids and we go into town. We could get those guitar strings and maybe have lunch at the diner and I could show you and the kids the joys and secrets of our little town."

The smile that lit her face nearly stole Luke's breath away. "That sounds nice," she agreed.

"Great, we can finalize the plans tomorrow or the next day when I'm here." He stepped off the porch.

"That sounds fine," she returned.

He nodded and waved, then hurried toward his truck, wondering what on earth had possessed him to issue such an invitation.

Chapter 8

It was a perfect day for an outing. Overnight a cool front had passed through, and the weathermen were forecasting a comfortable eighty degrees for the day's high temperature.

Abby tried not to dwell on the pleasure that swept through her as she discarded first one outfit, then another in an effort to dress for the trip into town. She couldn't help but look forward to spending the day in Luke's company.

She told herself it was because she had very little interaction with adults, that most of her days and nights were spent in the company of the children. It was only natural that she would be looking forward to a little adult conversation.

Looking at the clock and seeing it was a quarter to ten, she quickly decided to wear a pale pink sundress that she knew was both becoming and comfortable.

She checked her reflection in the bedroom dresser mirror, making sure her lipstick wasn't smudged and her hair was brushed, then left her room to make sure the kids were ready to go.

They sat in the living room on the sofa, wiggling and squirming with suppressed eagerness. Abby realized they were just as eager as she was for a trip into town. They had dressed themselves with care, and their faces were scrubbed shiny clean and their hair neatly brushed.

"You two look terrific," she exclaimed.

"You look pretty, too," Jason said, and Jessica nodded in agreement.

"Thank you, kind sir," she said and curtsied. "We'll be the best-looking family in Inferno today," she said, and the two kids giggled.

At that moment a knock fell on the front door, and Abby knew Luke had arrived. He'd finished the porch the day before, and the last thing he had done was open the front door so it was once again functioning. She opened the door to greet him, and her breath caught in her throat.

Always before, she'd seen him dressed for work, wearing worn jeans and faded T-shirts or jeans and no shirt. This morning he was again clad in a pair of tight jeans, but instead of his customary T-shirt, he was wearing a gray-and-black-striped dress shirt. The sleeves were rolled up to expose his strong forearms, and the colors of the shirt enhanced the black-lashed beauty of his eyes.

"Good morning," he said, his gaze sweeping over her with obvious approval. "Wow, you look terrific," he said, and the heat that flowed from his eyes caused a warmth to sweep into her cheeks.

"Thank you," she replied. "You look really nice, too."

He grinned. "When you go to town on a Saturday morning, it's good to clean up a bit. And I must say, Ms. Graham, you clean up damned fine."

Again heat suffused Abby's cheeks, and at that moment the kids pushed past her and flew out the door.

"Let's go!" Jason exclaimed. "We want to go shopping and eat lunch at the diner and see all the stores."

Luke laughed and gestured Abby out the door. "Looks like somebody is eager for a trip into town."

Abby locked the house, then stepped off the porch, following Luke and the kids, who were just ahead of her. "Where's your pickup?" she asked as she realized a beige station wagon awaited them.

"At the ranch. We use this to transport guests, and I figured it was better to drive it than have the kids ride in the back of the pickup." His eyes twinkled with humor. "Of course, if anyone sees me driving this thing, it's going to totally destroy my image. A black, shiny pickup is a babe magnet. A beige station wagon just isn't the same."

"I'll tell you what, if we see any babes along the way, you can duck down and I'll pretend like I'm driving."

Luke laughed.

Abby got into the front passenger seat while the kids got into the back. "Buckle up," she reminded them as Luke slid behind the wheel.

Within minutes they were on their way.

"Nice day," she said, fighting a wave of unaccountable shyness. She'd slept with this man, knew most all the parts of his body intimately and yet at the moment felt nervous and shy.

"Gorgeous," he agreed. "It's always nice when autumn brings cooler temperatures."

"I guess cooler is relative. Back home, autumn just meant the beginning of winter."

"That's one thing we don't have here," he replied. "The winter months are our best months at the ranch. We stay fully booked from November through February with people wanting to escape winter."

"It will sure be nice not to have to worry about shoveling snow or driving on icy roads." She settled back in the seat and tried to relax. "So, you mentioned the other day you're going to show us all the joys and secrets of Inferno. What kind of secrets are there?"

"Is there buried treasure?" Jason asked from the back seat.

Luke laughed, the deep rumble shooting pleasure through Abby. "Not that I know of, Jason. If I knew there was buried treasure somewhere in Inferno, I would have dug it up long ago."

Luke shot Abby a conspiratorial wink. "But I can show you real bullet holes in the side of the bank where a band of desperados tried to steal the bank's money."

"Wow," Jason exclaimed. "I can't wait to see that."

"And what are the holes really?" Abby asked,

keeping her voice low so Jason and Jessica couldn't hear her.

"Oh, they're real bullet holes, all right, but they weren't put there by desperados," Luke said, keeping his voice low, as well.

"So, how did they get there?" she asked, leaning slightly toward him in an effort to hear his quiet voice. Instantly she could smell the familiar scent of him, the woodsy, spicy male scent that had driven her half wild when she'd made love with him.

"Burt Holloway used to work as one of the tellers in the bank before he retired last year. One day his wife called him outside and held him at gunpoint against the side of the building. Seems she was miffed because she'd heard a rumor that he was flirting with one of the waitresses down at the Honky Tonk."

"So she shot him?" Abby asked incredulously.

"She unloaded a six-shooter into the wall behind him but didn't hurt him none. Just put a touch of fear into him. Old Burt, he hasn't been back to the Honky Tonk since."

"What are you guys whispering about?" Jason asked, a touch of indignation in his voice.

Luke wheeled into a parking space in front of the diner, shut off the car, then turned to look at Jason. "We were trying to decide if you were going to drink one or two chocolate shakes at lunch."

"Two!" Jason exclaimed.

"Then we'd better get sightseeing so we can work up an appetite," Luke said.

The four of them got out of the car, and Abby and

the kids looked at Luke for direction. "Let's see the bullet holes first," Jason said.

"Is that okay with you, Jessica?" Luke asked, his tone infinitely gentle with the little girl.

She nodded affirmatively and grabbed Abby's hand.

"Then we'll begin our tour of the lovely town of Inferno at the bank."

Minutes later the four of them stood in the alley beside the bank, eyeing the six holes in the adobe building. "What are desperados?" Jason asked curiously.

"Bank robbers...bad guys," Luke replied. "But don't worry buddy, bad guys go to jail."

"And they stay there forever?"

Jason's question hung in the air for a moment, and Luke looked at Abby, as if wanting help in answering the question. "Most of the time bad guys stay in jail forever," she replied, the tiny white lie told to still a little boy's fears.

"What you have to remember, Jason, is that we're the good guys," Luke said. "And the good guys always win." In one smooth movement he picked Jason up and placed him on his shoulders.

Jason squealed in delight as his arms locked beneath Luke's chin. "Look at me, I'm tall as a tree," he said and laughed.

And that set the tone for the day. Luke took them in and out of quaint little shops. He took them to the fire station manned by volunteers where the kids got to sit on the shiny red fire engine and play with a litter of kittens that had taken up residency there.

Everywhere they went Luke was greeted with

friendliness. It was obvious he was adored by the women of the town, and liked by the men, as well.

And throughout the town tour, Abby found herself fighting the enormous attraction that had drawn her to Luke from the moment she'd first met him.

It didn't help that he seemed to have endless patience with the kids. He was sweetly gentle with Jessica and abounding with good humor in the face of Jason's endless curiosity. And to Abby's surprise she found those traits sexy as hell.

She couldn't help but realize that this was the way a family interacted, that to strangers on the street who didn't know either her or Luke, they appeared to be a perfectly normal, happy family.

And she knew the danger of those kinds of thoughts. She hadn't lied to Luke when she'd told him she had learned to expect nothing from men.

Certainly Justin Cahill had shown her the epitome of cruel indifference, and Ken…he had simply shown her that words of love spoken when blue skies abounded meant nothing when stormy seas lay ahead.

At least Luke had been honest with her, telling her that in seven months he was out of there, and he had no intention of allowing anything or anyone to stop his pursuit of his dream.

It was midafternoon when they finally stopped for lunch at the diner. The meal was accompanied by lots of laughter as Jason pled his case, once more, for a dog.

"I would clean my room twice every day," Jason said. "And Jessica told me she would, too." Jessica nodded vigorously in eager agreement.

"And we'd make you breakfast on Saturdays...your favorite, pancakes. And if we had a dog, Jessica and me would feed him and take him outside for walks and take care of him so you wouldn't have to ever do anything. We'd do everything around the house and you could just stay in bed if you wanted and—"

"Whoa." Abby laughed and held up a hand to still the promise-spewing Jason. "I'll tell you what." She grabbed her purse and got out a handful of change. "Why don't you and Jessica go play the jukebox and let me think about it for a few minutes."

Jessica and Jason scrambled from the booth, leaving Abby and Luke alone for the first time that day. Luke smiled at her across the table. "You know they aren't going to be happy until you get them a dog."

"I know," Abby agreed with a small laugh. "Jason has been unrelenting in his quest, and there's a small part of me that thinks it wouldn't be such a bad thing. I mean, I know the bulk of the work for a pet would fall on my head. But on the other hand, having a dog seems so wonderfully normal and right."

"And you want wonderfully normal and right for the kids," he said.

She nodded. "I do."

He took a sip of his soda and gazed at the children, then back to her. "My offer still stands to help you find a good dog."

"You've done too much for me and the kids already," Abby replied.

"You keep wearing that killer dress and I'll keep trying to do nice things for you." His eyes glowed with a familiar heat that she hadn't seen since before they'd made love.

"And you keep looking at me like that and I'll try to do nice things for you," she returned, her voice slightly breathless.

He laughed, not the full-bodied laughter he'd shared with the kids all morning, but rather a low, seductive laugh that held a promise that momentarily swept away her ability to breathe.

She broke eye contact with him and grabbed her glass of water, her mouth suddenly achingly dry.

"You feel it, too, don't you, Abby?" His voice was whisper soft, and again she looked at him, into the heat of his sexy eyes.

"Feel what?"

He smiled knowingly. "The desire to repeat what we did the other day." Like powerful twin magnets, his eyes held hers, making it impossible for her to look away. "That dress is lovely on you, Abby, but all I've been able to think about all day long is taking it off you."

Flames of heat warmed her cheeks at his words. "I must say, that surprises me." She fought to control both her blush and the raging turmoil his words created.

He lifted a dark eyebrow. "And why should that surprise you?"

"If I am to believe that you are the womanizer people in this town have told me you are, then half the excitement of getting a woman in bed would be in the chase. I'm afraid I didn't give you much of a chase."

"Abby." He reached across the table and drew one

of her hands into his. "I'm the first one to admit that I like women and I've dated a lot of women. But I don't sleep with all the women I date and I definitely don't like to play the kind of head games so many people like to play."

"I don't play head games, either," she replied. "I just... I'm not very exciting and..."

He squeezed her hand to still whatever other protest she was about to make. "Abby, you have no idea how exciting I find you, and I'd like to make love with you again."

"Let's change the subject. You're making it difficult for me to think."

He grinned and released her hand. "Okay, tell me what you were doing before you started taking care of Jason and Jessica."

"My life was okay. I was a third grade teacher."

"That doesn't surprise me. It's obvious you love children. Okay, so during the day you were a teacher, and in the evenings?"

She shrugged. "I visited with Loretta and the kids a lot and I was dating a man named Ken Masters."

Luke's eyes were opaque. "Were you in love with him?"

"No." The answer came swiftly and with assurance. "I wanted to be in love and I tried to fool myself that I was in love with Ken. He was a high school coach and we had school in common. We attended school functions together, and it just seemed sort of natural that we'd eventually be together forever."

"But he let you down."

She nodded her head. "He was great initially in the

days immediately following Loretta's death. It wasn't until he realized I intended to keep the kids with me that he started to freak out.''

She paused a moment and took a sip of her tea, grateful that thoughts of Ken no longer hurt at all. ''He tried to talk me into putting them into foster care. He said they required more than I could give them, but what he meant was their presence in my life cramped his style. I realized then that I'd been fooling myself about my feelings for him. The easiest thing I've ever done in my life was tell him goodbye.''

Before he could respond, the kids returned to the table.

''So, do we get to have a dog?'' Jason asked eagerly.

Abby gestured the kids into the booth. Jason slid in next to Luke and Jessica next to her. She eyed them both soberly, grateful to be on less treacherous ground talking about a dog with the kids instead of the past or Luke's desire for her.

''I've given this a lot of thought, and I've decided that next week, if Luke could take us to some of the dog breeders he knows, then we'll see about getting a dog.''

Jason yelped with excitement, and Jessica clapped her hands together, her button eyes shining with delight.

''Oh boy, a dog! That's a lot better than a lizard,'' Jason exclaimed.

Abby checked her watch and realized it was almost three. She knew Luke played his guitar and sang at the Honky Tonk on Saturday nights and probably had other things he wanted to do besides spend all his free Saturday time with her and the kids.

"We probably should be getting back home," she said to Luke.

He checked his watch and nodded. "Yeah, I've got a few things to take care of before I go to work tonight." He stood and pulled out his wallet.

"Please, let me get lunch," she said, fumbling quickly in her purse.

"I'm not accustomed to my date paying my way," Luke protested.

"We aren't a date," Jason exclaimed.

Abby laughed. "That's right. We aren't a date, and I insist I pay in return for your fascinating tour of town."

Luke grinned easily and stuck his wallet back in his pocket. "I never argue with a headstrong woman."

Luke and the kids stood nearby while Abby paid for the meal, then together the four of them left the diner. They had just reached the car when Luke snapped his fingers. "Hey, we almost forgot what we came to town to get—the guitar strings."

"You said the man in the general store orders them for you?" Abby asked. She knew the general store was a couple of blocks away, and she could also tell that the kids were growing tired.

"Why don't you guys go ahead and get in the car. It will just take me a couple of minutes to run and get them," Luke suggested.

"Let's go in here and look," Jason said, pointing to the craft store in front of where they were parked.

"Okay, if you aren't in the car, then I'll know

you're in there," Luke said, then turned and began to walk in long, even strides away from them.

"All right, we'll take a peek around and by that time Luke will be back," Abby said as she guided the kids to the quaint shop's door.

Inside the air was cool and sweetly fragranced by candles and potpourri. The shelves held an array of items—knitted booties and crocheted blankets, hand-sewn dolls and wooden painted trucks.

There were hand-painted bird feeders and intricate yard ornaments, flower arrangements and paintings and cross-stitched towels and T-shirts.

"Hello...hello. Welcome to My Place." A dainty, gray-haired woman approached them, beaming a smile and bearing a platter full of cookies. "I'm Rita Sue Ellenbee, the proprietor of this establishment."

"Hi, I'm Abby Graham and these are my children, Jason and Jessica," Abby replied.

"Ah, yes, the town has been buzzing with the news of the pretty new widow and her lovely children. Would you like a cookie? My own special recipe of honey and oatmeal." Rita Sue held out the platter.

"None for me, thank you," Abby replied, then nodded at the kids, who each took one.

"Feel free to wander around. We have something for everyone in here."

"We're just waiting for Luke," Jason said around a mouthful of cookie.

"Luke? Luke Delaney?" Rita Sue asked, and Abby nodded.

"He's such a nice young man...a bit of the devil

in him, but just enough to make him fun. His work always sells the quickest here.''

''Really? What kind of things does Luke sell here?'' Abby asked curiously.

Rita Sue placed the platter of cookies on a shelf and gestured for Abby and the children to follow her. ''I haven't put out his newest work yet. He just dropped it off to me a couple of days ago.''

She led them into a back room that was obviously used for storage. Boxes and crates lined the walls, and in the center of the room set a gorgeous, solid oak dressing table. ''That's Luke's work,'' she said.

Abby ran her fingers across the smooth, glazed wood in surprise. ''It's beautiful,'' she said, awed by the workmanship displayed in the intricately carved lines and decorative etching. ''He's been doing some work for me around my place, but I had no idea he was so talented.''

''Luke could make a good living just building furniture, but he doesn't seem to have any real ambition that way,'' Rita Sue said. ''He brings me a piece every couple of months, and it usually sells the first day I put it out on the floor. I'm always harping at him to make them faster, but he just grins that devilish grin of his that tells me he's going to do it in his own time, his own way.''

Abby smiled. ''Thank you for showing it to me. And now we'd better get outside. Luke will be looking for us.''

They walked toward the front door, where a young couple was just entering. Rita Sue grabbed her platter of cookies and went to greet the new couple.

Abby gazed out the plate glass window as the kids stopped to look at a display of tissue-paper flowers. She didn't want Luke to have to come in search of them.

Main Street was busy, and it was obvious many people had come out to enjoy the pleasant day. Several men sat outside the barbershop on a bench, and a young couple walked leisurely hand-in-hand, apparently window-shopping.

At the corner, the sheriff stood chatting with another man, and as Abby's gaze swept over them, her blood froze and her breath.

No. Her mind screamed in denial as she stared at the man with the sheriff. It couldn't be. Her heart banged painfully in her chest.

She drew a deep breath and forced herself to calm down. She could only see the man's profile. She had to be mistaken. It couldn't be him...just somebody who resembled him.

"No," she whispered. No, it couldn't be him. Fate wouldn't be so cruel, and she had tried to be so very careful. When he turned, she'd see that it wasn't him at all.

Then he turned, and she saw him fully. It was him. Her heart once again boomed in frantic rhythm as her blood turned icy cold in her veins.

Somehow, some way, Justin Cahill, the man who had murdered her sister, the father of the children she claimed as her own, was here in Inferno.

And he could only be here for one reason. He knew they were here. He had found them.

Chapter 9

The minute Luke saw Abby sitting in the car, he knew something was wrong. She wasn't just pale—she looked positively ill.

The kids both seemed okay. They were buckled into the back seat, each of them looking at books Abby had bought for them earlier in the day.

But Abby definitely was not okay. He threw the guitar strings on the seat between them and slid behind the steering wheel. "What's going on?" he asked.

"Nothing. Everything is fine…just fine," she replied, a sharp edge in her voice. "I just really need to get home right away."

"All right, we're on our way." He started the engine and pulled away from the curb, aware of her gaze darting frantically out the front window, then out the side.

The tension rolling from her was thick enough to

cut, and he could hear her taking shallow little breaths, as if she were fighting off sheer hysteria. As they drove away from town, she constantly turned in her seat to check the road behind them.

"Abby, what's going on?" he asked again, unease rising in him as he recognized that the emotion that darkened her eyes appeared to be fear. "Did somebody say something to you? Did something happen while I was gone?"

"Is something wrong?" Jason asked from the back seat.

"No, honey. Everything is fine…just fine," Abby said to him. "I'll tell you later," she said in a low voice to Luke.

The drive was finished in silence. Abby continued to twist in her seat and look out the rear window as Luke tried to figure out what might have happened in the space of the few minutes he'd been getting the guitar strings.

When they reached the house, Abby opened the front door and told the kids to go inside and turn on the television or play in their rooms, then she stepped out on the porch with Luke.

Her eyes still held an edge of panic, and her delicate hands worried themselves, clenching and unclenching, twisting and wringing.

"I have to think," she said absently and paced the front porch. "We have to go…we have to leave here."

"What are you talking about?" He stepped closer to her and grabbed her hands in his. "What do you mean, leave here? Where are you going?"

"I don't know…we just…we just have to go. We

have to get out of here.'' Her hands were cold as ice and trembled unsteadily. She tried to pull them away, but he held on tight.

''Why? Why do you have to leave? For God's sake, Abby, tell me what's going on.''

Tears formed in her eyes as she gazed at him. ''I can't tell you. I can't tell anyone. I'm afraid...'' The tears trickled from her eyes and fell down her cheeks. ''Please, let me go so I can get the kids ready to leave. If we stay here, I'll lose everything, and the children will be lost.''

''I'm not going to let you go until you tell me what's going on.'' Luke squeezed her hands. ''Abby, you can trust me. Maybe I can help.''

She drew a deep breath. ''You can't help,'' she said with an edge of bitterness. ''Nobody can help.''

''Try me,'' Luke exclaimed. ''Trust me.'' He dropped her hands and grabbed her shoulders.

For a long moment she gazed into his eyes, as if assessing him to see if he was worth her trust. Finally, he felt the tension in her ebb slightly. ''Justin Cahill has found us.'' The words were whispered hoarsely as if torn from enormous force.

''Justin Cahill?''

''The kids' father.''

Luke frowned in confusion. ''But I thought...you said he'd disappeared.'' He dropped his hands from her shoulders.

''He's not disappeared anymore. He's here in Inferno, and he can only be here for one reason. He wants his children,'' she exclaimed, her voice laced with undisguised bitterness. ''I put all my faith in the judicial system, and it let me down." She moved to the porch railing and stared into the distance.

She looked so fragile, so small and helpless, Luke's heart ached for her. He moved to stand next to her. "What happened?"

"Justin was arrested for the murder of my sister, and I was granted temporary custody of the children. The murder case was handled by an overeager assistant district attorney. She charged Justin with first-degree murder and refused to consider including any lesser charges. She was so certain she'd get him."

"But she didn't."

Abby turned to face him, her eyes tortured pools of emotion. She worried a slender hand through her hair. "No, she didn't. In her defense, it looked like an open-and-shut case. After all, she had two little eyewitnesses to the crime, and even though Jason and Jessica were horribly traumatized, she was certain that by the time the trial took place they would be able to testify."

"But they weren't."

"Jessica quit talking altogether, and whenever Linda, that was the assistant DA, tried to talk to Jason, he'd fly into rages and tears. Finally I told her she couldn't use them, that she'd have to figure out the case without their testimony. She remained confident. They had Justin's fingerprints in Loretta's apartment and a neighbor's testimony that he'd thought he'd seen Justin lurking around just before the murder took place."

"And that wasn't enough to see him convicted?"

"At the last minute Justin produced an alibi witness for the time of the murder." Abby's voice rang with festering anger. "A young woman came forward to testify that Justin was with her the entire night of the murder. The case fell apart after that."

Once again she directed her attention to the distance, and her fist hit the porch railing in barely contained rage. "I had told Linda from the very beginning that first-degree murder wasn't the right charge. She couldn't prove premeditation, and I begged her to include lesser charges for the jurors to consider. But she didn't want to hear it. She was so damned confident that she could turn the jury her way."

"But she didn't," Luke concluded softly.

All the anger, all the bitterness seemed to fall away from her, leaving her looking painfully vulnerable, achingly defenseless. "No, she didn't."

As Abby's eyes filled once again with tears, Luke drew her into his arms and held her tight.

"Two months ago the verdict came in…a hung jury, a mistrial. I was at my apartment with the kids when Linda called to give me the bad news." She shuddered, her voice muffled by his chest. "And Linda told me unless new information came to light, they weren't going to try him again. I knew the moment he got released he'd come looking for me… come looking for his kids. So I packed up and ran, and I've been running every since."

She lifted her head and through the haze of her tears a steely strength shone. "By taking the kids and running, I know I broke the law. But I had no other choice. I will not allow him to have Jason and Jessica. He's a brutal, hateful man, and he'll destroy them. I had to break the law in order to save them from him.

He's a murderer, and he only wants them for two reasons—actually, two million and one reasons.''

"Two million and one?"

She nodded and stepped out of his embrace. "First and foremost, I know he wants them to make sure they continue their silence about the night of Loretta's death. But the main reason he wants them in his custody is that each of them has a trust fund of a little over a million dollars apiece."

Luke whistled, shock sweeping through him. "I guess that gives him a little over two million reasons to want to be a good daddy."

"Justin was never a good daddy," she said, her eyes flashing with a renewed burst of anger. "He was cold, and brutal, and authoritarian. The kids were terrified of him before the night he killed my sister, and I'll do whatever it takes to make sure they stay safe from him." Once again she threaded her fingers through her hair, then turned toward the front door. "I can't waste any more time. I've got to get the kids packed, and we need to get out of here."

She started for the door, but Luke stopped her by grabbing her arm. "So that's it? You just run?"

"That's right," she replied, her chin raised in mute defiance.

"And when he finds you again?"

"We run again…and we keep running until we find a place where he won't be able to find us." Her chin went a notch higher. "I don't care how many laws I have to break to keep those babies safe."

"And what kind of a life is that for your kids?"

The chin that had a mere moment before been raised

in stubborn bravado lowered, and her eyes flickered with a haunting deep pain. "It's better than what Justin will give them," she said softly, her voice quivering with the depth of her emotion.

"But is it good enough? Always in hiding, afraid if Justin doesn't find you the law will? What kind of a life is that?"

She attempted to jerk her arm from his grasp. She obviously didn't want to hear what he had to say, but he held tight. "Abby, there's got to be another way. You can't condemn those kids to a life on the run."

"I tried the other way," she cried and this time managed to tear her arm from his grip. "I trusted the system to do the right thing, to put him in prison and keep him away from the children. But it failed me. It failed them. The day he walked out of that courtroom acquitted, he regained the right to have his children. And he's a murderer. He beat my sister to death in a fit of rage!"

"But the children have a right to have a normal life, with a permanent home and the same school, the same friends and a dog."

A sob caught in her throat as she slumped against the front door, utter defeat on her features. "Don't you think I know that? Don't you think I want that for them? But I don't know what to do. Justin could show up here at any minute and demand I give him his children, and legally, he'd have that right."

Luke had never wanted to help anyone more than he wanted to help her and the children at that moment. "Maybe it's time you stand and fight."

She sniffled and straightened. "But I have no tools, no weapons to fight him."

"Yes, you do," Luke protested. "You have two very powerful tools. You have Jason and Jessica. Even though they might not be ready or willing to talk about the night of their mother's murder, surely they'd be willing to tell a judge they want to remain living with you. And I happen to be related to the best lawyer in the state, my sister, Johnna. I can call her right now, and she'll start the ball rolling in getting you permanent custody."

For the first time since they'd left town, a tiny ray of hope shone from her eyes. Once again Luke placed his hands on her shoulders, felt the warmth of her sunkissed skin beneath his fingertips. "Abby, stay. Fight. Give Jessica and Jason a chance for a normal childhood.

Luke wasn't sure why, but it suddenly seemed overwhelmingly important that the children got the opportunity to have good childhoods, the kind Luke had never had.

"You'll call your sister?" she said, the first real sign that she was contemplating his words.

"Right now, if you want me to."

Again tears welled in her eyes. "I'm so scared, not for me, but for Jessica and Jason."

He pulled her to his chest, and she came willingly into his embrace. He stroked a hand through the shiny silk of her hair and hoped to hell he hadn't just given her the worst advice in the world.

The attractive woman with boyishly short dark hair flew through the front door when Abby opened it, bringing with her a dynamic energy that Abby found oddly comforting. "Johnna McCain," she said and grabbed Abby's hand in a strong grasp.

"I'm Abby. Abby Graham."

"Nice to meet you, Abby." Johnna's gaze shot to her brother, who was seated on the sofa. "You said it was an emergency, so I got here as fast as I could."

"Please, have a seat," Abby said as she gestured Johnna toward the chair across from the sofa. As she sat, Abby sank down on the sofa next to Luke, her nerves raw and on edge.

For the past hour, while they'd waited for Johnna to arrive, Abby had expected at any moment a knock on the door and the unwelcome presence of Justin Cahill demanding his children.

She was also more afraid than she'd ever been in her life that she was making a bad decision, trusting when she should be running. What if she didn't win this fight? What if this was the biggest mistake she'd ever made in her life?

"So, what's going on?" Johnna asked, looking first at Abby, then at Luke. "What's the big emergency?"

Abby drew a deep breath and for the second time that day bared the secrets that had driven her actions for the past two months. She told Johnna about the debacle of a trial, how when the verdict of a mistrial had been announced, Abby had packed the kids up and spent the next six weeks traveling from motel to motel, seeking anonymity and safety.

After six weeks, disheartened by the lifestyle of constantly being on the move and living out of boxes and suitcases, Abby had remembered her inheritance from her crazy uncle Arthur and had come here.

"Didn't you think Justin Cahill might be able to trace you here?" Johnna asked as she looked up from the notes she'd been taking on a legal pad.

"Uncle Arthur died when Justin was already in jail. This place was left to Loretta and me, and since Loretta was dead, it all became mine. I didn't think Justin knew anything about the inheritance."

"Apparently he learned something, otherwise there would be no reason for him to be in Inferno," Luke said.

"Where is Justin's home? Where were you all living when the crime occurred?"

Abby was grateful for the way Johnna phrased the question. It was easier to think of it as the crime than the murder of her sister. "We were all living in Kansas City, Missouri." She shot an apologetic look at Luke. "I told you Chicago, but that was a lie."

He nodded, appearing unsurprised by this information.

"Okay, let me get this straight," Johnna said. "Legally you were granted temporary custody when Justin was arrested and put into jail."

"That's right," Abby replied.

"And legally, you have received no notice that the temporary custody was terminated."

"No, nothing. But it would have been difficult for me to get notice since we were on the run."

Johnna nodded and took a moment to make several more notes on her pad. "The first thing I'll need to do is check to see if anything has been filed in the state of Missouri. I want to get the trial record and take a look at that…see if there's anything I might use in a custody battle."

She looked at Abby. "I have to ask you a question that might make you angry, but I need all the facts if I'm going to help you."

"What question?" Abby asked, tensing in preparation for something unpleasant.

"You told me these kids have over a million dollars a piece in a trust fund. I need to know what your financial status is. I need to make sure that Justin Cahill can't use the fact that you're after the children's money and that's the only reason you want custody."

Abby nodded, unsurprised by the question and pleased she had an answer that would erase any argument that might be made concerning her motives for gaining custody. "I have my own trust fund, more than both of the children put together and more than I could ever spend in a lifetime." She smiled self-consciously. "My father was something of a financial wizard and wanted to make sure we were all taken care of."

"Great," Johnna exclaimed. "You have some sort of documentation of that?"

Abby rose from her chair and went into the kitchen, where she grabbed her purse off the table. She returned to the living room and withdrew a business card from her wallet.

"This is my lawyer in Kansas City. He's the executor of the trust funds. I'll contact him and tell him to send you any pertinent paperwork. I haven't accessed any of my money since we left Kansas City. I was afraid of leaving any kind of a paper trail that Justin might try to follow. But apparently he found us anyway.''

Luke reached out and grabbed her hand as he heard the wealth of emotion in her voice. "You're doing the right thing," he said, as if he'd heard the doubts swirling around in her head.

She nodded, although she was no longer certain what the right thing was. She was putting her children's safety and well-being in the hands of a woman she'd never met before today and a man she'd made love with, but didn't know much better.

"What kind of work does Justin do? Can he physically provide a stable environment for the children?"

Abby frowned. "He never held down a job when he was married to Loretta. I know he was beneficiary of a small insurance policy, and I suppose when he was found not guilty he got that, but he probably has a wealth of attorney fees to pay." Abby shrugged helplessly. "I don't even know where he might be living now. When he and Loretta split, he was living in a small studio apartment."

"Okay," Johnna said. "I'll get my investigator checking into his background and find out what ammunition we can use." She closed her pad and eyed Abby somberly. "Unfortunately, I can't do anything about this until Monday morning. First thing Monday I'll file the paperwork requesting permanent custody of the children."

She stood, and Abby and Luke did the same. "I have to be honest here with you, Abby. Family courts generally like to keep kids with their biological parents. But I'm a fighter, and it's obvious you are, too.''

Abby and Luke walked with her toward the front door. ''I'll do my damnedest to make sure those kids remain with you. In the meantime, if Justin shows up here, under no circumstances do you allow him to have the children. Call Sheriff Broder and tell him at the present time you have legal custody.''

''Don't worry,'' Abby said. ''There's no way I'd allow him the kids.''

At that moment Jason called Abby from his room, where he and Jessica had been playing. Abby smiled at Johnna. ''And speaking of kids, I better go see what's going on.''

Johnna nodded. ''Too bad you aren't married. Family court also loves two-parent families. Go...'' She waved Abby away. ''Go see to the kids. Luke will see me out the door.''

Abby nodded and hurried down the hallway, aware that she had just set into motion a battle of mammoth proportions. She was gambling, and the stakes were high, the well-being of the two children she loved more than anything else in the world. She had to win. If she didn't, they would all be destroyed.

Chapter 10

"What are you doing, brother?" Johnna asked as she and Luke stepped out of the house.

"What do you mean?"

"Playing Sir Galahad is not your usual style," Johnna said dryly.

"Maybe I'm changing my style," Luke replied more sharply than he intended. He drew a deep breath to steady the emotions that had rolled through him from the moment Abby had spilled her secrets. "She's a very nice lady, and she needs help."

"And you talked her into getting help."

He hesitated, then nodded. "She was set to run again."

"But you convinced her to stand and fight." Johnna's gaze lingered on him thoughtfully. "Are you involved with her?"

He shrugged, breaking eye contact. "Sure, I've

been doing some work for her around the place. I built her the new porch, and she wants her kitchen cabinets replaced.''

Johnna elbowed him in the ribs. ''You know that's not what I meant.''

''What difference does it make?'' he asked as they reached her car.

''I was wondering what might happen if you talked her into staying and fighting, then I lose the custody battle.''

Luke smiled at his sister, a smile that held little humor. ''Then I guess you'd just better be sure you win the battle.''

''Sure, no pressure there.'' Johnna opened her car door, but instead of getting in she turned to face Luke. ''Be careful, Luke. Abby seems nice enough, but she's trouble. I can tell you that if everything she told us is true, this custody battle has the potential to get very ugly. You don't need to get yourself involved in something like this. You're fighting your own personal demons.''

Luke looked into the distance, knowing his sister was talking about his drinking problem. ''At the moment the happiness of those kids seems a lot more important than a drink. They have suffered enough. All I want is for them to get a chance to have a normal, happy childhood.''

He turned to Johnna as she placed a warm hand on his arm. ''The kind of childhood we never had?'' Her gray eyes were filled with emotion, and Luke knew she was remembering the kinds of horror they'd suffered at the hands of their abusive father.

"Yeah, something like that," he finally replied.

Again Johnna studied him, her brow creased thoughtfully. "You know, Luke, by fixing their childhood you won't be fixing your own."

"I know that," he scoffed, uncomfortable by her piercing gaze and speculative expression. "What is this? Psychology one-oh-one? I'm just trying to help out a woman who is alone and trying to do something good for a couple of kids. Don't make it into any more than that."

"Okay." Johnna dropped her hand from his arm but remained standing next to her car. Her gaze swept around the area. "It's kind of isolated out here, isn't it?"

"Yeah, it is."

Johnna frowned. "Maybe I should get in touch with Judd and see if he'll kind of keep on eye on things out here until we get something legal going on. If Justin Cahill has killed once in the heat of anger, there's nothing that says he won't kill again to get what he wants."

Judd Walker was the private investigator Johnna used in her law practice. "No, that's okay. I'll take care of it," Luke said. "I'll stick around here until we've got a handle on Cahill."

Johnna reached up and laid a palm on Luke's cheek. "Be careful, Luke. I don't want to see you getting hurt."

She didn't wait for his reply, but got into her car and started the engine. As she drove away from the house, Luke stared after her.

Johnna had been angry for as long as Luke could

remember, rebelling against the cruelty of their father, railing about the injustice of their lives. But somehow when she'd married Jerrod McCain a month before, she'd found a kind of peace.

It was as if in Jerrod's love, she'd found self-worth and the ability to put the past firmly behind her. And in doing that, she was becoming a softer, more caring person.

Luke raked a hand through his hair and stared at the sun, which had begun its descent. Things were changing. His sister and brother Mark had changed. It unsettled Luke.

He turned and faced the house, thinking of what Johnna had said. He'd put in motion events that might ultimately lead to Abby's destruction. And how would he feel if that happened and she looked at him with dead eyes, or with eyes filled with blame?

What difference did it make, he asked himself. Abigail Graham meant nothing to him. They'd made love and spent some time together, but it wasn't like he intended to have any kind of a long-term relationship. In seven months he'd be gone from here.

Still, the thought of her losing the kids to the man who had killed their mother, the man who had killed Abby's sister, tore through him. If she lost the kids it would be his fault because he'd encouraged her to stay and fight.

He dragged his hand down the side of his face, trying not to think that he might be instrumental in Abby's ultimate undoing. He had to think positive. He'd help her through this and do anything to help Johnna and Abby win the battle for the kids.

With this thought in mind, he went to his truck and retrieved the guitar strings he'd bought, then walked into the house. He found Abby in the kitchen preparing the evening meal. She flashed him a surprised, taut smile. "I thought you'd left with your sister."

"What made you think that?" He tossed the strings onto a countertop.

She dropped an unwrapped package of hot dogs into a pot of boiling water. "You have to play tonight. I figured you'd need to get going in order to make it to the Honky Tonk on time."

"I'm not going to play at the Honky Tonk tonight." He sank down in a chair at the table. "In fact, I'm not going anywhere tonight."

Her dark, perfect eyebrows rose in confusion. "What do you mean?"

"I mean I'm going to stay here for a few days. I don't want you here alone with just the kids in case Justin shows up."

"I can't ask you to do that, Luke," she protested weakly.

"You didn't ask, and I insist," he replied. "Don't worry, everything will be aboveboard. I'll bunk on the sofa."

"I'm not going to protest," she said, and turned to the stove to stir a pan of beans. "To tell the truth, Justin has always scared me more than a little bit. I don't want to be here alone if he shows up."

Luke saw the tense set of her shoulders, knew the emotions that had to be rolling through her. Panic, uncertainty, fear... She had to be experiencing them all.

He shoved back from the table and moved to stand behind her. He placed his hands on her shoulders, and she stopped stirring the beans and leaned back just a little bit.

"You're going to win this, Abby," he said softly. "Johnna is smart and tenacious, and she'll use every tool at her disposal to win for you."

She turned to face him, her eyes sparkly bright with unshed tears. "I hope you're right. I can't imagine what their life would be with him. And I can't imagine my life without them."

At that moment Jason and Jessica raced into the kitchen, and Luke dropped his hands from Abby's shoulders. "We're starving," Jason exclaimed.

"Then I guess we'd better eat," Abby exclaimed with what Luke knew was forced cheerfulness. "Jason, why don't you get the plates and set the table. Jessica, you do the silverware and the napkins."

"And what about me?" Luke asked.

"Drinks," Jason replied. "You can get us something to drink for supper."

They all worked for a few minutes in silence, then sat down at the table to enjoy a simple meal of hot dogs, beans and potato chips.

Jason provided suppertime chatter, recapping their time spent in town as if none of his three dinner companions had been with him.

Abby and Jessica were silent, and Luke worked overtime to fill the dead silences, rattling about the dude ranch and all the horses they owned.

Abby's tension didn't seem to dissipate throughout the meal. When the supper dishes were done, she called the two kids into the living room. She sat on the sofa and motioned for Jason to sit on one side of her and Jessica on the other. Luke realized she had to tell the children something of what was going on.

Thinking she needed some time alone with them, he excused himself and stepped out on the front porch. Night had fallen, and silence reigned. The sky, as usual was clear, filled with the sparkling of thousands of stars.

Luke leaned against the porch railing and stared into the thick blanket of darkness that surrounded the house. He was vaguely surprised Justin Cahill hadn't shown up. It wouldn't take the man long to find out where the new woman in town lived.

Maybe Abby had been wrong. Maybe it hadn't been Justin, after all, just a man who'd resembled him. Maybe she'd panicked over nothing.

And maybe Justin Cahill was biding his time, setting up an offensive assault, secure in the fact that Abby didn't know he was anywhere near her and the kids.

It was difficult to believe a day that had been so good could be transformed into such a mess. Luke had enjoyed their trip into town and had been taunted and teased by Abby's loveliness throughout the day.

She'd been a vision in that pink sundress that had emphasized her small waist and displayed her slender, shapely legs. He'd been on a slow sizzle all day, but the sizzle had been effectively doused by the appearance of Justin Cahill back in her life.

He'd been leaning against the porch railing for

about a half an hour when the front door opened and Abby stepped outside.

"How did it go?" he asked.

She shrugged. "They're frightened, but I did my best to reassure them. I couldn't not tell them. What if Justin does show up here? I didn't want them to be taken by surprise."

She moved to stand next to him, and instantly the sizzle was back. Her scent surrounded him, and her body heat radiated toward him. "What are they doing now?" he asked, trying to concentrate on anything that would take his mind off his desire to take her in his arms and kiss her.

"Getting ready for bed." She sighed, a whisper soft sound of weariness.

"It's been a long day, hasn't it?" Again he had to fight his impulse to embrace her, to pull her tight against his chest. She didn't need any further complications at the moment, and he certainly was savvy enough to know that now wasn't the time for sex or romance.

"Yes, it has been." She turned to face him, her eyes luminous in the moonlight that spilled down. "And I never thanked you for what was a lovely trip into town."

He shrugged and jammed his hands into his pockets. "You don't have to thank me. I thoroughly enjoyed myself."

"I just can't believe this is happening. I guess I should have never come here. I should have driven into Mexico and started a new life there."

"But then you wouldn't have had the good fortune

of meeting me.'' Although Luke's voice was filled with teasing humor, she didn't respond but merely uttered another weary sigh.

They stood in silence for several long minutes, and Luke wondered if she sensed his growing need to touch her. The moonlight loved her features, the soft glow appearing to magically erase any tension.

She sighed one last time and rippled her hair with her fingertips. ''I'd better get the kids tucked in.''

''If you have a chance to get that guitar for me, I'll be glad to string it this evening.''

She nodded and disappeared inside. Luke followed a moment later. He sank down on the sofa and closed his eyes, listening to the soothing sounds of her voice drifting from Jason's room.

His mind played and replayed the conversation with his sister. What were the odds of them winning custody for Abby? Certainly Luke knew enough about the law to understand that if Justin Cahill had been found not guilty in Loretta's murder, then they couldn't use the murder as a reason for a judge to terminate his parental rights.

But surely a judge couldn't ignore the expression of fear in the kids' eyes at the mere mention of their father. Surely their desire would be taken into consideration.

He snapped his eyes open as Abby came into the living room, the old guitar in one hand and a set of sheets in the other. A pillow was tucked under one arm.

He jumped up, grabbed the bedding from her and set it on the coffee table. ''I didn't know if you'd need a blanket or not,'' she said. ''The house stays fairly warm at night.''

''This is fine,'' he assured her, then grinned. ''I'm an old, seasoned cowboy. I've got my horse to keep me warm.'' He didn't realize how much he'd missed her smile until it flashed, bright and carefree, for a brief moment.

''Just keep your horse outside. I'm having enough problems contemplating a dog in the house.'' Her smile disappeared as quickly as it had come. ''And now, if you don't mind, I think I'm going to call it a night. I'm more than exhausted.'' She placed the guitar on the coffee table next to his bedding.

''Go on, get a good sleep. Things will look better in the morning.''

''Do you promise?''

Those green eyes of hers held his, and more than anything he wanted to promise her that morning sun would bring hope and happiness. ''I told you once that I don't make promises I can't keep. To be perfectly honest, I don't know if things will look better in the morning or not.''

She smiled again. ''Thank you, Luke.''

''For what? For telling you tomorrow might be just as crappy as today?''

''For everything. For being kind and for staying here and for making me see that a life on the run isn't what the kids need.'' Again for a long moment her gaze held his, and he thought she wanted to say something more…or needed something more from him. Then she broke the gaze and turned away. ''Good night, Luke. I'll see you in the morning.''

She disappeared down the hallway and into her room. Luke watched her go, then went into the kitchen to retrieve the strings he'd tossed on the countertop earlier. Before leaving the kitchen, he checked the back door to make sure it was securely locked.

He returned to the living room, grateful for any task to take his mind off everything that had happened that afternoon. Before he began to string the guitar, he checked the front door, as well, to make sure it was locked up tight.

He sat on the sofa and began to string the guitar, his thoughts whirling chaotically in his head. Surely Justin Cahill wouldn't be foolish enough to try to take the children by force.

He'd want to present himself as a poor, beleaguered man who'd been wrongly accused of his ex-wife's death, acquitted of the crime and now wanting, needing to be reunited with his children.

His role as victim wouldn't work if he stormed this place and took his children by force.

It didn't take Luke long to string the guitar, then he worked on tuning it, strumming the strings softly so as not to disturb the other occupants in the house. When the guitar was tuned to his satisfaction, he placed it on the coffee table and set about making his bed for the night.

Keeping in mind that there were two kids in the house, he decided to sleep in his jeans. In the morning they'd all have to take a trip to the ranch so Luke could get some spare clothes.

Luke yawned, surprised to find himself exhausted. Normally on a Saturday night he'd play at the Honky

Tonk until three in the morning, but on this Saturday night he was exhausted despite the fact that it was just a few minutes after ten.

Within minutes of keeping his eyes closed, he fell asleep.

A scream awoke him. He sat straight up, for a moment disoriented as to his surroundings and what had pulled him from his sleep. A sliver of moonlight slid through the windows, and as he looked around the room he remembered. He was at Abby's.

The scream came again, a familiar, high-pitched expression of abject terror. Jason. Luke sprang from the sofa and raced down the hallway to the little boy's room.

Abby was already there, and just like last time Jason's arms and legs were flailing wildly as he suffered the throes of an unspeakable nightmare.

"Shh, baby, it's all right. I'm right here," Abby said as she fought to control Jason's gyrations.

This time, instead of giving Abby an opportunity to send him away, Luke strode into the bedroom and sat on the end of the bed. Gently but firmly, he grasped Jason's ankles so the little boy couldn't kick Abby and she could concentrate on dodging his windmilling arms as she tried to wrench him from his nightmare dreamscape.

"Jason, sweetie, wake up. It's just a dream. You're safe here."

Within minutes Jason had awakened and sobbed in Abby's arms. "I don't want to live with my daddy," he cried. "I want to stay here with you forever."

"And that's exactly what you're going to do,"

Abby assured him. "Don't you worry, Jason. I'm going to do everything I can to make sure that you live with me forever."

Luke remained seated on the foot of the bed as Abby stroked Jason's brow and attempted to send the little boy back into a peaceful slumber.

She was a terrific mother. Luke's admiration for Abby fluttered through him. These kids needed her. They needed her patience and her love. And he once again silently vowed to do anything it took to help her win her case.

As the minutes passed, Luke became aware of several things, like the fact that Abby's sweet scent filled the room and that she was clad only in a pale pink frilly nightgown.

With the light shining from the night-light in a nearby wall socket, the gown almost appeared translucent. Luke couldn't tell if he could really see the faint, dark circles of her nipples beneath the thin fabric or if it was just his imagination.

He knew every inch of her, had lovingly studied her body the single time they had made love, but now he had an overwhelming desire to learn every inch of her body all over again.

His body reacted to his thoughts, filling with a tension that seemed almost unbearable. But it was a tension he wouldn't, couldn't follow through on.

He'd told her that everything would be aboveboard, that he would sleep on the sofa. He couldn't very well tell her he'd prefer to sleep in her bed each night and make love to her from dusk until dawn. He couldn't very well tell her he'd really like to ease the tension that simmered in him by kissing her, touching her, making slow, sweet love to her.

He stood, and with a nod to Abby left the bedroom. He turned on the lamp on the coffee table in the living room and sat down on the sofa, too wired to fall back asleep just yet.

Picking up the guitar, he willed the tension to leave his body, willed away the desire that had momentarily struck him. He strummed the strings in a soft, melodic tune, allowing the music to physically relax him even as his mind whirled.

Apparently Abby's talk with the children had stirred the demons in Jason's head, resulting in another of his nightmares.

Luke knew all about nightmares. He'd suffered horrendous dreams until he was about thirteen years old. In his dreams he hadn't been fighting to protect his mother against his father, but rather himself. He'd dreamed often that his father was trying to kill him and suffered the knowledge that if his father succeeded, nobody would care.

He mentally shook himself to dispel thoughts of his miserable childhood and instead thought over the conversation he and Abby had had with Johnna earlier that evening.

The most difficult thing for Luke to accept was that he was as helpless in this situation as he'd been as a young child dealing with his father. What he wanted to do was fix it, fix the whole thing so Abby would be happy, fix it so the kids would be assured a good life.

He set the guitar down as Abby came into the living

room. She'd pulled on a short coral-colored terry robe that was belted tightly at her slender waist.

"I finally got him back to sleep," she said. She stood in the doorway between the hall and the living room, looking as fragile as Luke had ever seen her.

And in that instant, something Johnna had said replayed in his mind and he knew exactly what he wanted to do. It wouldn't solve the problem, but it might just give her a fighting chance.

"Abby." He stood and faced her. "Marry me."

Chapter 11

"Excuse me?" Abby wondered if the stress of the day coupled with a lack of sleep had affected her ability to hear accurately.

"Marry me."

Luke strode over to where she stood and took her hands in his. He pulled her to the sofa, where they both sat. "Think about it, Abby. You heard Johnna this evening. She said it was too bad you weren't married, that judges liked to put children in stable two-parent homes. So let's make this a two-parent home."

She pulled her hands from his, her head reeling with his crazy suggestion. And it was crazy…wasn't it? "Luke, I…that's crazy," she finally managed to say.

"What's crazy about it?" His gray eyes bore into hers intently. "We get married and fight for custody. Once the custody battle is decided, then we have an amicable divorce. You get the kids, and I go to Nashville. Everybody goes away happy.''

Abby frowned, finding it hard to think with him sitting so close to her, with his naked, muscular chest inches away from her. Everybody goes away happy, he'd said, and she'd love to believe that it was exactly what was going to happen.

But could she ask this man to give up his single status, even temporarily, for her? Confusion whirled in her head, and she felt the dull throb of a headache at the base of her skull. She stared at the coffee table, unsure what to do, what to say.

''Abby, this might provide the edge that you desperately need,'' Luke continued. She looked at him once again, saw in his eyes a burning need she wasn't sure she understood.

She rose. ''I need to think about it,'' she said. She offered him a faint smile. ''Your offer has thrown me for a loop. This is too important to decide at a moment's notice. I need some time to assess things.''

He nodded. ''Go to bed. We can talk about it in the morning.''

Abby drew a deep breath. ''Yes, we'll talk about it in the morning.'' She murmured a good-night, then went into her bedroom and crawled into bed.

She'd hoped that sleep would claim her quickly, but it remained elusive as she tossed and turned, thinking and rethinking everything that had happened during the day.

She thought of Jason's terror and Jessica's silence. She thought of how much she had grown to love the two kids, how much she wanted to shower them with the love she would never get a chance to give her dead sister.

More than anything, she wanted to protect them… protect them from the kind of life they'd have with their father. Loretta had been married to Justin for six years at the time of her murder, and in those six years Abby had learned enough about Justin Cahill to know he was dangerous.

As she'd stood at the grave, burying the sister she'd so loved, she'd vowed to herself that she would do anything to make certain the kids never had to live with that man again.

But did *anything* mean a temporary marriage to a man she didn't know that well? Would a marriage to Luke really help her or hurt her in the end?

"Okay, I'll marry you," she said the next morning as she walked into the kitchen and found Luke seated at the table with a mug of coffee before him. "Unless, of course, you've changed your mind," she hurriedly added.

He grinned and pointed her to the chair opposite him. "Sit," he commanded. "I think it's only right that I pour a cup of coffee for my wife-to-be."

"Are you sure about this, Luke?" she asked as she sat at the table.

"I've never been more sure about anything in my life," he replied.

She watched as he poured her a cup of coffee. It was obvious he was freshly showered—the scent of fresh soap hung in the air, and his hair was still slightly damp.

He set a mug of the hot brew in front of her, then

returned to his chair across from her. "Don't look so scared," he said. "I promise you a temporary marriage to me won't be too painful."

She smiled and wrapped her hands around her mug. "I want you to understand that if we do this I won't expect anything from you. I mean, it won't be like we'll be a real husband and wife."

"You mean you promise you won't henpeck me or make me account for every hour I'm away from you, or spend all my money on foolish female things?"

She laughed, his teasing tone calming her nerves and oddly enough shooting strength through her. Her laughter died and she eyed him somberly. "But I'm serious, Luke. If we do this I want you to understand that I don't want you to change your lifestyle in any way. I will expect nothing from you during or after the marriage."

"Okay," he agreed easily.

"And I don't think we should say too much about this in front of the kids. I don't want to confuse them. I mean, I don't want them to think that you are going to be a part of their lives forever." She felt a blush warm her cheeks and knew she wasn't making the point she'd intended to make. She looked into her coffee mug. "Just so as not to confuse them, I think the sleeping arrangements should remain the same even after the wedding ceremony."

"Okay." Once again he agreed easily, and she looked at him gratefully, only to see the charming, devilish sparkle in his eyes. "But I have to warn you, that doesn't mean I'm not going to try to talk you into a conjugal visit once in a while."

Abby's cheeks grew hotter, and she was saved from having to make a reply by the appearance of the kids. It wasn't until after breakfast, when the kids had gone outside to play, that she and Luke got a chance to talk alone once again.

"I spoke with Johnna while you were dressing the kids," Luke said, patting the sofa next to him for her to sit. "I told her what we have planned and made the arrangements to meet her and Jerrod at the church at noon tomorrow."

"Noon tomorrow?" Abby echoed faintly and sank down beside him. Suddenly it seemed so real, and she felt a nervous fluttering in her stomach. In less than twenty-four hours she would be Mrs. Luke Delaney.

"Johnna is going to take the kids into a playroom at the church while her husband, Jerrod, performs the ceremony. My brother Mark and his wife, April, will be our witnesses, and as far as all of them are concerned, this is a love match, not a temporary arrangement."

Abby looked at him in surprise. "But don't you want your family to know the truth?"

He shook his head. "I don't want anyone to know the truth. I don't want a whisper of this to get to Justin. As far as everyone in this town is concerned, you bowled me over with your charm, captivated me with those luscious green eyes of yours."

"And remind me again what I'm supposed to tell everyone when they ask why I married you," she said teasingly.

He leaned toward her, his eyes bewitching, his smile the sexy one that shot heat through her. "You can tell everyone that I stole your heart one night when we danced together under the stars.''

Abby's heart stepped up its rhythm as she worked to think of something fun and sassy to say in return. But her mouth was too dry to speak as her head filled with the magic of those moments when they'd danced together in the moonlight.

Luke reached out a hand and ran his fingertips down the side of her jawline and across the hollow of her throat. His touch was warm and soft and sent a shiver racing up Abby's spine.

She forced a light laugh and leaned away from him. ''I think I'll tell them that I felt sorry for you.''

He sat up straighter and eyed her in surprise. ''Sorry for me?''

She nodded. ''Because before you met me you were just drifting through life without a purpose, without knowing real happiness, and I came along and saved you from yourself and your wayward lifestyle.''

He laughed. ''Ah, so you're one of those rescuing women.''

''Not really,'' she replied more soberly. ''There are only two people on this earth I really want to rescue…Jason and Jessica.''

Luke leaned toward her once again and laid a hand against her cheek. ''I know,'' he said softly.

Suddenly Abby needed to get away from him, gain some physical distance. ''And speaking of the kids,'' she said as she jumped up from the sofa. ''I'd better go check on them.''

A few moments later, she breathed deeply of the mid-morning air as she watched the kids playing on the tire swing. The emotions that whirled inside her confused her.

She had once believed herself head over heels in love with Ken Masters, but Ken had never made her feel the way Luke did. And she certainly wasn't in love with Luke Delaney.

She was just feeling an exceptional amount of warmth toward Luke because of what he was doing for her and the kids. Surely that explained the way her heart fluttered at his merest touch, the way her pulse stepped up its pace when he looked at her.

It was intense gratefulness she felt toward Luke, and nothing more. After all, the man who had professed to love her with all his heart had walked out on her when she'd taken custody of the kids. And Luke, a man who didn't even pretend to love her, was willing to go the extra mile in order to try to help the children she so loved. Of course she'd be feeling grateful and warm toward him.

At eleven the next morning, Abby, Luke and the kids headed into town. Their first stop was the courthouse, where Abby and Luke obtained their marriage license.

"I can't believe you can get a license and get married all in the same day," Abby said as they got into the car to drive to the church.

"We don't believe in wasting time in Arizona, so there's no waiting period," Luke replied.

Within minutes they were at the church, and Abby fought a wave of nervousness that was nearly nauseating. Everything had happened so quickly. She almost wished there were a waiting period in Arizona so she would have time to think…to make sure that she was doing the best thing for everyone.

Johnna greeted them at the door of the small, quaint-looking church. She introduced them to her handsome husband, Jerrod, the minister who was going to perform the ceremony, then whisked the kids away to a back room where she said she had all kinds of fun awaiting them.

"We'll just wait a few minutes for Mark and April to arrive," Jerrod said.

"Is there someplace where I can freshen up a little?" Abby asked, trying to still the nerves that jangled inside her.

Jerrod pointed the way to the ladies' rest room, and Abby slid inside the door, grateful for a few moments alone. She stared at her reflection in the mirror above the sink. The pale-faced bride-to-be who returned her stare was a stranger.

Was she doing the right thing? There had been no word from Justin, although Johnna's private investigator had confirmed that he was, indeed, in town. Still, he'd made no move to contact Abby or the children.

Maybe they were jumping the gun. Maybe they were overreacting to the situation. Maybe this whole wedding thing was not necessary.

A vision of Jason's face, of Jessica's face exploded in her mind, and she knew it was impossible for anyone to be overreacting where their safety was concerned. Justin's silence was ominous, and she couldn't fool herself into thinking otherwise.

She smoothed her hands down the sides of her dress. For her wedding gown, she'd chosen a knee-length, sleeveless beige dress. It was cotton, nothing real fancy, but she'd never worn it before and felt it was perfect for a simple wedding ceremony.

And Luke...Luke looked magnificent in a pair of charcoal dress slacks and a white shirt. They had gone the day before to his family ranch so he could pick up clean clothes. There, Abby had met his oldest brother, Matthew. Matthew had been curt but civil and obviously surprised by the news that his baby brother was getting married.

Luke. His name rang inside her, creating a heat that had no source. He'd teasingly told her he would do his best to talk her into a conjugal visit or two, and she wasn't sure he would have to talk too hard to get what he wanted.

"Abby?" Luke called to her through the door. "Mark and April are here. It's time."

It was time. Time for her to temporarily bind herself to Luke. She would become his wife in the eyes of the law and before God, but she had to remember that her marriage wouldn't last until death did them part...but would end in seven months when Luke left Inferno forever.

She left the rest room and was greeted by Luke, who introduced her to his brother Mark and Mark's pretty wife, April.

April took Abby's hands in hers and smiled warmly. "I'm so pleased," she said. "Luke is a wonderful, warm, caring man, and I'm so pleased you were able to see beneath his facade and find and fall in love with the man within."

Abby made what she hoped was an appropriate response, enormous guilt sweeping through her. She wanted to confess to April that this wasn't really a marriage of love, but rather a marriage of survival—her children's survival. But she knew Luke was right. Nobody must know the truth until the custody issue was settled.

"Every bride needs some flowers," Luke said, and

surprised her by handing her a nosegay of sweet-smelling baby white roses.

"How did you manage this?" she asked, the gesture touching her more deeply than she cared to admit.

He grinned. "I have my ways."

With Jerrod orchestrating, they all got into their positions, April standing next to Abby and Mark standing next to Luke in front of the small altar.

A sense of numbness swept through Abby as Jerrod began speaking the words that would make her and Luke husband and wife.

She'd once dreamed of this moment, of a long white dress and a lacy veil, of splendid flowers and golden bands. Most of all, she'd dreamed that her wedding would be the beginning of a lifetime of love and passion and laughter.

Maybe someday she would still have her dream wedding, but at the moment she was binding herself to Luke in a temporary arrangement in the best interests of Jessica and Jason.

"Will you join hands and face one another," Jerrod instructed.

Abby's cold, slightly trembling hands were clasped in Luke's bigger hands. The warmth and strength that radiated from his hands somewhat calmed the nerves that danced inside her.

She looked into his dark-lashed, smoky eyes and repeated the vows that would make him her husband. As she said the words, she was struck with a sense of horror as a jolt of realization struck her. There was more than a little bit of her heart that wished this was for real…forever. There was more than just a little bit of her heart that was in love with Luke Delaney.

As Luke said his vows, he knew the mixed emotions that had to be fluttering inside Abby. Her eyes were windows to those emotions, first darkening with a hint of anxiety, then lighting and sparking with something that pulled a ball of emotion into Luke's chest.

For the first time in his life, Luke felt as if he were doing something that was positively right. If he did nothing else for the rest of his life, at least he would have the knowledge that he put himself on the line to help two innocent kids. And that made him more than the loser his father had always proclaimed him to be.

It was crazy, but as he spoke the promise to love, honor and cherish Abby, he felt the words deep in his heart, deep in his soul. The emotion in his chest grew to mammoth proportions. Although he knew the vows they spoke were only temporary, he silently vowed to do whatever he could for Abby and her children for the time he would be in their lives.

"You may kiss your bride," Jerrod said, bringing Luke back to the moment at hand.

Once again he gazed deeply into Abby's eyes as he leaned forward to deliver the kiss that would seal their bond. Although the kiss was swift and light, the feel of her sweet lips beneath his sent a wave of heat cascading through him.

With the ceremony done, there were congratulations all around, then Luke and Abby gathered the children and left the church.

"I've got a surprise for us all," he said when they were in Abby's car after the ceremony had been completed.

"A surprise? What kind of a surprise?" Jason leaned over the seat.

"Sit back and buckle up and I'll tell you," Luke

replied. Jason did as he requested, and Luke continued, "How would you all like to go on a picnic?"

"A picnic? Cool!" Jason replied.

"I've got everything we need for a successful picnic
in the trunk," Luke said, then grinned at Abby who
was looking at him in surprise. "I was busy early this
morning while you were still in bed."

"A picnic sounds nice," she agreed.

"I'm going to take you to one of my most favorite
places in the world," he said softly. "It's a perfect
place for a wedding day picnic."

She smiled and nodded, then cast her gaze out the
car window. She'd been unusually quiet since the ceremony, and he wished he could read her thoughts,
wondered if she was already regretting their decision.

She looked as pretty as he'd ever seen her. The
beige dress was a perfect foil for her shiny dark hair
and displayed her slender curves to perfection.

His wife. Under the laws of the land and in the state
of Arizona, he'd just bound his life with hers, promised to love and honor her in sickness and in health,
until death do them part. Or until the custody issue
was resolved, he reminded himself.

He'd planned the picnic because he thought that
with the tension of the last two days, a little relaxation
and fun would be good for her.

It was another beautiful day, warm but not overly
hot. A faint breeze stirred the trees as Luke turned onto
Delaney property. He drove past the main house and
the guest cabins, following a dirt road into a pasture.

"Look, I see horses," Jason exclaimed. "Look, Jessica, there's a black one and a brown one."

"That's Mabel and Betty," Luke said. "We don't
ride them anymore. They've been retired, but maybe

later we can coax them over here to get a bit of an apple.''

He pulled in near a grove of trees and parked the car, and they all got out. Luke popped open the trunk and began to unload the items he'd packed earlier.

''A blanket, a basket of food, a ball, a Frisbee...'' Abby smiled at him. ''It would seem you've thought of everything.''

''I believe in the Boy Scout motto, be prepared.''

''Were you a Boy Scout?''

''Nah, I got kicked out of Boy Scouts for playing with the Girl Scouts,'' he teased. He was rewarded with her laughter. ''Jason,'' he called. ''Heads up.'' He threw him the ball, then tossed the Frisbee to Jessica.

While the two children played, he and Abby spread the blanket beneath a shady tree. ''Stretch out here and relax and I'll unpack the food,'' he said.

With Abby sitting on the blanket, Luke began to unload what he'd packed for their lunch. ''I hope you don't mind that I raided your refrigerator,'' he said. ''We've got balogna and cheese sandwiches, chips, apples and cookies.''

She tilted her head and eyed him curiously. ''You must have been up before dawn.''

He nodded. ''Prewedding jitters, I guess.''

As he pulled out a blue plastic container, she placed her hand on his arm. ''Are you sorry we went through with it?'' Her eyes, the beautiful green of spring, were filled with concern.

He leaned over and touched her cheek. ''Now how can I be sorry about marrying the prettiest woman in Arizona?'' he teased, then realized she wanted, needed more than that. He pointed to where the children were throwing the Frisbee back and forth.

"How can I be sorry for trying to help them? How can I be sorry for stepping up to the plate when all my life I wish somebody had done that for me?"

Her eyes held a compassion that made a curious ache in his chest. "I wish I would have been there for you, saved you from your mean, wicked father."

Luke smiled, consciously shoving aside all thoughts of his past. "I survived." He pulled a dark blue bowl covered with foil out of the basket. "And your kids are not only going to survive, they are going to thrive under your love and care."

Her eyes darkened. "I hope so. It's been three days and there's been no word from Justin. I don't understand why he hasn't contacted me yet."

"Conversation about that man is strictly off-limits today," Luke replied. "We aren't going to let him ruin our picnic."

She drew a deep breath. "You're right." She pointed to the blue plastic bowl. "What's in there?"

"It's a surprise. You'll see later." He set the bowl aside and called the kids to eat.

As they all sat on the blanket and enjoyed the food Luke had packed, their laughter ringing through the trees, Luke felt a strange sense of peace. He could see the main house in the distance, the house that had held his childhood bogeyman, and it was strange to him that the unhappiness he'd experienced there, at the moment, seemed distant and long ago.

It was as if Jason's boyish, braying laughter and Jessica's sweet little giggles chased away the ghosts of his past.

As they ate, to the delight of the children, Mabel

and Betty drew closer. When Jason and Jessica had finished eating, Luke cut up a couple of apples into horse-bite-size pieces.

"Just go stand in front of them and hold a piece of apple out in your hand and they'll take it from you," Luke instructed. "Don't worry, they won't hurt you." Jason led the way, Jessica hiding behind him as they approached the horses with the apples.

"And now, dear Abby, I told you once what the best way to eat strawberries was...." He popped the top of the bowl to display ripe, red strawberries.

Abby's face lit with surprise. "Where did you get them?" she asked in obvious amazement.

He grinned, pleased that she was pleased. "I raided them from the ranch yesterday when we came to pick up my clothes. Now, stretch out and let me feed them to you one luscious berry at a time."

"Luke," she protested with a charming blush. "It isn't necessary that you feed me."

"Ah, but it is." He took one of her hands and gently pushed against her shoulder, guiding her down to the blanket on her back. "I promise to be a good and dutiful husband for the duration of our marriage if you'll just indulge me this one whim."

Her eyes twinkled merrily. "And this is the only whim of yours I'll have to indulge?"

Heat swept through Luke as he thought of all the whims he would like them to indulge together. He stretched out on his side next to her, the bowl of strawberries between them.

Jason and Jessica had finished feeding the horses and were playing a game of hide-and-seek as Luke fed Abby the first plump, juicy berry.

The moment her mouth closed not only around the

berry, but the tip of his finger, as well, Luke knew he was in trouble. White-hot desire swept through him.

He fed her another strawberry, unable to speak as he worked to staunch the flow of heated blood through his body. Abby seemed to sense his sudden mood change from teasing to tormented.

Her eyes deepened in color, and once again a blush stained her cheeks. Her lips were rosy red with berry juice, and what Luke wanted to do more than anything was kiss her long and hard.

"Oh, boy, strawberries." Jason's delight tore Luke from his growing fog of desire. "Can me and Jessica have some?"

"Sure," Luke agreed and sat up. Abby also rose to a sitting position. He wondered if she had any idea how precariously close he'd come to losing it...how he was both grateful and disappointed that Jason had quelled the mood of the moment.

The four of them polished off the strawberries in no time. But it wasn't until the sun was slowly sinking in the sky that they packed up and headed back to the house.

As they drove home, they sang old childhood songs. Jessica didn't sing, but clapped her hands in rhythm, her eyes sparkling with happiness.

It had been a good day. The issue of the custody battle ahead, the specter of Justin Cahill had remained at bay for the duration.

They'd ended their time in the pasture by the four of them playing Frisbee. Abby had kicked off her high heels and taken off her panty hose, then chased after the flying disc like a wood nymph chasing a butterfly.

She placed a hand on his arm, her eyes sparkling. "Thank you, Luke. It was an absolutely perfect day."

"It was nice, wasn't it?"

"And I know two little people who will sleep very well tonight," she added.

Luke nodded. He knew one good-size man who would probably sleep quite poorly. He wondered how many newlywed grooms spent their wedding night alone on a sofa.

But this wasn't really a marriage, and he wasn't really a groom, he reminded himself. They had entered into this arrangement for the children. Abby wasn't in love with him, and he certainly wasn't in love with her.

"I can't believe how much the kids took to the horses," Abby said, breaking into his thoughts.

"Next week, we'll take them over to the ranch and let them ride. We'll ride in the morning, then take the afternoon to find that dog you've promised them."

Luke had never expected such mundane things like a promised horseback ride and finding the perfect dog would bring him a sense of joy. But he was actually looking forward to them. He could easily imagine Jason and Jessica's faces the first time they were put on the back of a horse or the first time their new dog licked them.

"Let's sing Bingo," Jason said from the back seat, and once again the car rang with song and laughter.

All laughter died as they pulled into Abby's driveway and saw a patrol car waiting there. "Oh, no, what now?" Abby said softly.

Luke parked the car and they all got out.

"Evening," Sheriff Jeffrey Broder greeted them, his features set in sober lines.

"Sheriff." Luke nodded, then spoke to Abby.

"Why don't you go open the door and let the kids go on in the house."

She nodded, lines of tension that had been gone all day appearing on her lovely face.

"What's up?" Luke asked the sheriff softly as Abby went to unlock the front door.

"I hate like hell to be out here," Broder said. "But you know part of my job is serving papers for the county."

"So, you're here to serve papers?"

Broder nodded, then offered Abby a tight smile as she rejoined the two men. "Abigail Graham?"

She nodded, trembling like a leaf precariously clinging to a tree in a stiff wind. Luke placed an arm around her shoulders.

Jeffrey held out a large, official-looking envelope. "You are hereby served."

Abby took the envelope from him but didn't open it right away.

"On a more pleasant note, I hear congratulations are in order," Jeffrey said. He offered a gentle smile to Abby. "Maybe your influence can keep this guy out of my jail."

Abby shot Luke a surprised glance.

Luke smiled. "Don't worry, I'm not a habitual lawbreaker. There's been a couple of times that Jeffrey allowed me the use of one of his jail cells to sleep off the effects of too much alcohol, but that was a long time ago."

"It has been a long time," Jeffrey agreed. He shifted from one foot to the other, obviously uncomfortable. "Well, I guess I'll just get out of here. Again, my congratulations on your marriage. I never thought you'd bite the bullet, Luke."

"Me, neither," Luke replied and pulled Abby closer against his side. "It took one very special woman to capture me."

Luke held tight to Abby even after Jeffrey's car had disappeared into the distance. Her fingers trembled as she opened the envelope and pulled out the legal papers that told them Justin Cahill was attempting to legally reclaim his parental rights to his children.

And so, the battle had begun.

Chapter 12

"This is where we stand so far," Johnna said to Luke and Abby. It was Wednesday morning, and the three of them sat at Abby's kitchen table. "Judd has been terrific in getting us good information on Justin Cahill. Right now we know he's staying at Rose's Bed and Breakfast in town."

"Maybe we could get Rose to poison those homemade muffins she offers her guests in the mornings," Luke said dryly.

Abby smiled at him. "Or at least short sheet his bed," she replied.

Luke returned her smile, and she felt a rivulet of warmth flood through her. It frightened her just a little, how much she'd come to depend on his strength, on his sense of humor and on his neverending optimism in getting through all this.

Johnna ignored their little asides and continued.

"Judd has learned that Justin has no visible means of support. He lives in a small, one-bedroom apartment in Kansas City and he's a loud complainer about how the judicial system screwed up his life with false murder charges."

"So right now Abby and I have the upper hand as far as where is the best physical place for the children to be," Luke said.

"That's true," Johnna agreed. "But that could change at any moment. All Justin has to do is tell the judge that he intends to get a bigger apartment or rent a house. Judd was able to get into his bank records and has discovered that Justin is not rolling in the dough, but he's certainly not destitute."

"Who is this Judd?" Abby asked.

"He works as a private investigator for me," Johnna explained.

"He's in his mid-thirties, moved to Inferno a couple of years ago," Luke explained further. "All anyone really knows about him is that he's a loner, used to work for the FBI and lives like a hermit in an old house on the north side of town."

"Justin has retained the services of Gordon Clemens, an attorney from Tucson. He's supposed to be a real shark."

Abby's heart fell. "Can you handle him?" she asked Johnna.

Johnna flashed her a full grin. "I eat sharks for breakfast. Now this is what's going to happen. We've filed all the appropriate paperwork, and I've talked to a children's services social worker to line up a home study."

"What exactly does that mean?" Luke asked.

"Her name is Sonya Watkins and she's going to come out here Saturday morning and look around the place. She'll speak with both you and Abby and talk to the kids." Johnna placed the woman's business card on the table. "Her report will hold a lot of weight with the judge. And we have a court date in two weeks."

"So quickly?" Abby shot a panicked gaze to Johnna.

"The quicker, the better, Abby," Johnna said gently. "You don't want this hanging over your head... over the kids' heads. We're a small county, and unlike the rest of the country, our children's services department isn't overworked. And I think that's it for now," Johnna said, and closed the folder in front of her.

She stood, and Luke and Abby did the same. "I think it's obvious that Justin intends to use the court system to get what he wants and has no intention of storming this place to take his kids by force."

"Good luck if he tries," Luke said grimly as the three of them walked to the front door.

"Oh, and something else," Johnna said. "I think it's best if you stay away from the Honky Tonk until this is all settled," she said to Luke. "We'll play up the ranch and your woodworking abilities to the judge."

"I'd already made that decision," Luke said. "Although I have to play there this Friday night for just a couple of hours. It's Jim Grogin's birthday, and I promised him months ago that I would sing a couple of his favorite tunes at his party at the bar that night."

Johnna frowned. "Okay, but after that, stay away from that dive. And for goodness sake, Friday night, don't do anything stupid." She flashed a smile at Abby. "I'll be in touch." And with that, she flew out the door.

Abby turned to look at Luke and instantly realized he was angry. A pulse throbbed in his tensed jaw muscles. "Luke? What's wrong?"

She followed him to the sofa, where they both sat. "Nothing," he said, his voice curt.

She placed a hand on his thigh. "Luke, you've been so good the last couple of days listening to my fears, my sorrows, almost everything that is in my heart. Why won't you share with me what has your jaw twisted into knots and your hands clenched into fists?"

He sighed and raked a hand through his thick, dark hair. "I just get so irritated because my sister and my two brothers always seem to expect the worst from me. It irritates me that they don't believe in me."

"But I believe in you," she said softly.

He turned to look at her, his eyes deep pools of smoldering flames…flames that threatened to instantly consume her.

He didn't say a word, but rather took her in his arms and captured her lips in a hot, hungry kiss. Just that quickly, they were out of control.

From the moment he'd fed her those strawberries on the blanket in the pasture, in the back of Abby's mind she'd yearned to make love with him once again.

And she'd known it had been on his mind, as well. She'd seen the hunger in his eyes when he gazed at her, felt the electricity flowing from him when their hands brushed or their shoulders bumped.

In the instant their lips met, any and all reasons they shouldn't make love again fled Abby's mind. All she knew, all she could comprehend was the hunger for his touch, her need for his body against hers.

He deepened the kiss, his tongue touching hers as his hands tangled in her hair. As he pressed her closer she could feel his heartbeat banging, racing in rhythm with her own. And she could feel his obvious arousal.

"Abby, sweet Abby," he murmured as his lips left hers and trailed down the side of her jaw to the sensitive skin just below her earlobe.

He gently tugged her hair, tilting her head back to give him better access to the hollow of her throat.

His mouth nipped and kissed, shooting fire through her, filling her with a heat she knew only he could stanch. He raised his head to look at her, to see the assent in her eyes, then he stood and scooped her into his arms and carried her into her bedroom.

Johnna had arrived early enough that morning that Abby hadn't had an opportunity to make the beds. Luke deposited her gently in the middle of the jumbled sheets, then stepped back and pulled his T-shirt over his head.

As Luke undressed, Abby did the same, driven by a fever of need, of want. She wanted to be naked with him, for him. She wanted immediate skin-to-skin contact.

When he joined her on the bed, she moaned in pleasure as his warm flesh made contact with hers and she was surrounded by that woodsy, spicy scent that always drove her half-wild.

He gathered her into his arms, the hairs on his chest teasing her nipples, the length of his legs wrapping around hers. Once again his mouth sought hers in a kiss of fiery intensity.

When the kiss ended, his eyes bore into hers. "I feel as if I've been on fire for months...years...and the only thing that can put the fire out is you."

"I've felt the same way," she replied, her voice husky to her own ears. She tangled her fingers in his hair and pulled him closer for another kiss, lost in splendid sensual pleasure, lost to everything but the magic of Luke.

And it was magic...every stroke of his hands, each touch of his lips created an enchantment that momentarily swept away all the cares of the world, banished all fear and uncertainty.

Time seemed to stand still as he stroked the length of her body in slow, languid, torturously wonderful caresses. His mouth found every erogenous zone, lingering here and there to bring her the most exquisite pleasure.

He took her to the peak over and over again, but held back giving her the ultimate release. Over and over again he left her trembling with need, until finally he paused to put on a condom, then entered her.

Slowly, he moved deep within her, then pulled back slightly, hot friction sending Abby again to the peak of pleasure. Again and again Luke repeated the give and take, stepping up the rhythm as his breaths became short and shallow.

She felt Luke's rising tension, felt his muscles growing more taut, his body filled with immense heat that only served to enflame Abby.

As Luke cried out her name and stiffened against her, she tumbled over the edge, every nerve ending in her body tingling in splendid delight as she gasped breathlessly.

For long minutes afterward they lay in one another's arms, in an embrace so close Abby could feel Luke's heartbeat slowly resuming a normal rhythm.

"I'm sorry Johnna upset you," Abby finally said as she lay with her head on his chest.

He stroked a hand down her hair and drew a deep sigh. "She upset me because she reminded me that I'm probably an alcoholic."

Abby raised her head and looked at him. Despite the sunshine pouring into the room, his eyes were dark with more than a hint of self-loathing. "But Luke, you haven't drunk the whole time I've known you."

"I'm a recovering alcoholic, and Johnna's words just reminded me that I'll always be only one drink away from failure."

Abby placed a hand on his jaw. "But until you take that drink, you are a success. And I know you're brave enough, smart enough to stay strong."

He grinned, the darkness in his eyes lifting. "You are something else, Mrs. Abigail Delaney. I think in the next couple of days I'm going to build you the most beautiful kitchen cabinets in the entire state of Arizona."

"Luke, you don't have to do that," she protested.

He smiled again. "I know I don't, but I want to."

"I can pay you for your work," she said. "Now that Justin knows where I'm at, there's no reason for me to not access my trust fund."

"I don't want your money," he replied. "It will be enough for me to know that when I'm in Nashville, you and the kids will be living in a place that's nice." He pulled her to his chest and stroked her hair. "But for the moment I just want to stay here with you in my arms."

When I'm in Nashville. His words swirled around in her head, filling her with a profound sadness. She knew she shouldn't be sad. She'd gone into this arrangement with her eyes wide open.

Luke had never promised to love her, to set aside his dreams of singing for her and the children. He'd never promised to spend the rest of his life with her. He was here only until the custody battle was decided.

Two weeks. Johnna had said the trial was set for two weeks. There was both pleasure and pain in the short waiting period. She was glad the custody issue would be over, that she didn't have to wait an eternity to find out if she would be able to raise the children she loved.

Two weeks. It wasn't enough time for her to spend with Luke. She wanted more. She was in love with Luke and she wanted a lifetime with him.

She wouldn't make love to him again, knew that to do so would just make it that much more difficult when the time came to tell him goodbye. And she would have to tell him goodbye.

In six and a half months he would leave Inferno, but in two weeks he would leave her. She squeezed her eyes tightly closed against a sudden burning of tears.

She wasn't sure what was worse—the possibility that in two weeks she would lose the children or the absolute certainty that in two weeks she would lose Luke.

"I really hate to leave you and the kids," Luke said as he and Abby stood on the front porch. The sun was dying in the west, splashing the horizon with vivid colors.

"But you promised you'd do this," Abby replied. "We'll be okay, Luke. Justin hasn't shown hide nor hair around here. There's no reason to believe he'll suddenly make an appearance."

"I know, but I still don't like it." Luke sighed, his gaze lingering on Abby. "I wish I hadn't promised Jim Grogin that I'd sing tonight." He wondered if there would come a day when he tired of looking at her, when the scent of her didn't stir him to distraction.

"But you did promise." She reached up and straightened his collar, then brushed a piece of lint from the navy shirt he wore. "This Jim Grogin is a friend of yours?"

"He was a peer of my father's. When I was thirteen, he talked my father into letting me work a couple hours a day at his ranch. I don't think he really needed me, but I think he knew I needed a couple hours a day to escape from my old man."

Once again Luke directed his gaze away from her and toward the quickly setting sun. "He's a good man, and those hours I spent on his ranch were good ones."

It was a vast understatement. Jim was quick to praise the young Luke, and it was Jim who had taught Luke a love of wood and the basic elements of wood-working.

"Anyway, the six months I worked for him were the happiest months of my adolescence."

Abby tilted her head slightly and looked at him curiously. "Why only six months?"

"My father refused to let me work for him any longer than that. I think my old man saw that I was developing some pride and some independence, and he wasn't about to let that happen."

"Then it's important that you go. And if you don't leave now you'll be late." She smiled at him. "I swear we'll be fine here until you get home."

"I've got my key, so lock up tight and don't open the door for anybody. If you hear anything odd, anything at all, don't hesitate to call Sheriff Broder. He can be out here in minutes."

"Would you get out of here?" She laughed and gave him a nudge to move him off the porch.

"I'll be home by midnight," he said as he walked backward toward his truck.

"I'm sure the kids and I will be asleep, but Peaches will greet you with her puppy enthusiasm."

Luke grinned, waved, then got into his truck. On Wednesday afternoon when the kids had gotten out of school, Luke had taken Abby and the kids to a dog breeder he knew. There they had discovered Peaches, an eight-week-old golden retriever who had greeted Jessica and Jason as if they were long-lost best friends.

Peaches had come home with them, along with a

bag of dog food, water and food dish and a large cage for housebreaking and nighttime sleeping.

When the two kids had fought over who got Peaches in their bedroom for the night, it was decided that Peaches' cage would stay in the living room with Luke.

Three days that week, Abby had gone with Luke to the ranch so he could get his twenty-five hours for the week in. She spent the hours sitting at a picnic table in the shade, watching the guests and reading a book.

However, it wasn't the dog or working at the family ranch that was on Luke's mind as he drove toward the Honky Tonk. He was nervous about leaving Abby alone.

There was absolutely no reason for him to be nervous. Justin had given no indication that he intended to do anything but battle them in a court of law, so there was really no reason to be worried.

It felt strange to be worried about somebody else. Luke had spent all his life until this point not worrying about anyone. But Abby pulled out of him feelings he'd never felt before.

Still, that certainly didn't change his plans for himself. He was going to be somebody, become somebody important. In six and a half months, he'd be gone from here, on his way to his destiny.

He parked his truck in the lot in front of the Honky Tonk. For a moment he sat and stared at the gawdy neon sign, the dusty, smoke-filled curtains that hung in the window. He hoped this was one of the last dives he'd ever have to work, that when he got to Nashville he'd be working better places.

He also knew this place was one of his greatest temptations. The moment he walked through the doors, he'd smell the booze in the air, get that old sweet yearning as each and every bottle in the place sang a siren song.

He thought of Abby's words, of her assurance that he was strong enough to make good choices. Funny, but he wanted to make good choices for her. He wanted to be a better man...for her. Sighing, he got out of the truck, slightly disturbed by thoughts of Abby.

Although it was only a few minutes before nine, the place was already jumping. As Luke grabbed his guitar from the back of his truck and headed toward the front door, music drifted out along with the sounds of raucous laughter and the clinking of beer bottles.

Luke entered the large, dimly lit bar and was greeted by half a dozen of the regular customers. He returned their greetings as he wove his way through the crowd toward the tiny stage.

The guest of honor, Jim Grogin, was seated with his wife and grown children at the table just in front of the stage. He stood as he saw Luke approach. "Luke, I'm so glad you could make it," he said as he slapped Luke on the back. "When I heard that you'd gone and gotten yourself married, I wasn't sure you'd be here at all."

"I wouldn't miss it," Luke replied, and smiled warmly at the gray-haired man. He nodded to Jim's wife, Sadie, and to their two sons and their wives. "Looks like you've got the whole gang here."

Jim nodded. "All except the grandbabies." His pale

blue eyes twinkled merrily. "Can't have my sweet grandbabies in a dive like this."

"And the only way he got me into this dive is by promising me I would get to hear you sing," Sadie said.

"Let me buy you a drink, son," Jim said, and motioned for the waitress. "What will it be?" he asked. "As I recall, you used to be a Scotch man."

"Used to be, but now I'm strictly a soda man. I'll take a ginger ale," he told the cute little waitress.

"So, tell me about the woman who finally managed to capture your heart," Jim said. "I haven't seen her, but I heard through the grapevine that she's quite a looker with long dark hair and blue eyes."

"Green," Luke corrected. "Her eyes are green." He smiled as he thought of those lovely green eyes. He'd learned to watch her eyes, knowing that her moods and feelings would be reflected there. She would make a terrible poker player—her eyes would never allow her to bluff.

"And I understand she's got a couple of children," Jim continued. "I got a feeling she couldn't have picked a better stepdad for her babies. You learned firsthand about bad fathers. I got a feeling you're going to be a great one."

His words filled Luke with a crazy kind of guilt. He wanted to confess to Jim that fatherhood wasn't part of the deal, that the whole marriage thing was merely temporary. Instead he excused himself, telling them he needed to get set up and ready to perform.

Setting up required little more than positioning the microphone and a chair in place on the stage. He'd just finished doing that when the waitress came with his drink. "Just put it there on the edge of the stage," he said, then did a quick tune-up of his guitar.

It was nearly ten when Luke began his first set. He sang for twenty minutes, singing songs requested by people who yelled out their favorites.

He set his guitar aside, downed his soda and grinned at the waitress, who instantly replaced it with a fresh one. He took a ten-minute break, visiting with people who had become acquaintances over the years, then he began another set that included a rousing version of "Happy Birthday" for the guest of honor.

He was into his third set when he noticed the stranger watching him intently from the back of the room. Although Abby had never given him a physical description of Justin Cahill, Luke instantly recognized him. Jason and Jessica had the dark eyes of their father and the same cheekbones and slender face.

The man had the shoulders of a steroid freak, thick and bulging, made more apparent by the tank top he wore. There was a challenging glint in his dark eyes as he held Luke's gaze from across the room.

Luke was unsurprised when he finished the set and Justin Cahill stood at the foot of the stage. "Thought it was time I introduced myself to you. I'm Justin Cahill." He held his hand out for a shake.

Luke looked at his hand, the hand that Abby believed had killed her sister, and he deliberately shoved his own hands deep into his pockets.

Justin's eyes flared with the heat of suppressed rage. "So that's the way it is," he said tightly.

"It would appear that's the way it is," Luke replied.

Justin took a step toward him, invading Luke's personal space, but Luke didn't give the man the satisfaction of stepping back. "I just thought I'd stop by and let you know that there is no way in hell you're getting my kids. They belong to me."

Not "with me" but rather "to me." A definite indication that the man had no right to have his children. "We'll just have to wait and see about that, won't we?" Luke replied, refusing to rise to the man's baiting tone.

"I'm just giving you a friendly heads-up. I don't intend to lose this fight." With those final words Justin spun on his heels and headed for the exit.

Luke grabbed his soda and downed it, feeling as if he needed to wash a very bad taste out of his mouth. He set the empty glass down and headed for the back office of the tavern, where he knew there was a telephone.

"Toby, can I use the phone?" he asked the owner of the Honky Tonk, who sat at his desk going over paperwork.

"Help yourself." Toby waved toward the phone on the corner of the desk, not taking his gaze from his work.

Luke grabbed the receiver and quickly dialed. "Abby," he said when he heard her voice at the other end of the line. "Justin was just in here and just left. That means he knows you and the kids are there alone. He probably won't bother you, but I'm leaving here now and should be there in fifteen minutes."

"I'll keep the doors locked until I hear your voice," Abby said.

"Trouble?" Toby asked.

"Nothing I can't handle," Luke replied. "Would you do me a favor and lock up my guitar? I'm just going to sneak out the back door."

"Sure, no problem," Toby replied.

Luke started out of the office, but hesitated in the doorway, a wave of dizziness overtaking him. He shook his head, thinking he must have moved too fast, then headed out the back door.

He stepped into the night air, and the ground seemed to be moving, twisting and undulating beneath his feet. He slammed his back against the building and closed his eyes, drawing deep breaths and fighting against the blackness he sensed descending.

His drink. Justin must have put something in his drink. He shook his head again and took several steps forward. The blackness reached out, insidiously pulling Luke in.

Abby, his mind cried. It was his last conscious thought.

Chapter 13

Abby sat in the darkened living room staring out the front window, watching for Luke's truck. The house was quiet around her except for an occasional tiny whine from Peaches in her cage.

It had been almost thirty minutes since Luke had called, and she expected to see the headlights of his truck at any moment.

Luke hadn't gone into any real detail about seeing Justin, and curiosity burned inside her as she wondered what had happened, what had been said between the two men.

Peaches whined again, and Abby made her way through the darkness to the cage. "What's the matter, baby?" she asked softly. The dog nudged her cold, wet nose against her hand.

She knew if the light were on she would be able to see Peaches' beautiful liquid brown eyes gazing at her adoringly. She opened the cage, lifted the puppy into her arms and was instantly rewarded with a wet lick along her neck.

She returned to her chair and put Peaches on her lap. The dog wiggled and squirmed for a moment, then settled down, snuggling against her with a sigh of contentment.

As Abby returned her gaze to the window, she stroked the silky fur. The dog had already wrought a miracle of sorts earlier that evening. As the two kids were playing with her in the living room, Abby had heard Jessica tell the dog she loved her.

"I love you, Peaches," Jessica had said loud and clear. The first words Abby had heard her speak since her mother's murder. Abby hadn't said anything, hadn't even indicated she'd heard, but her heart had expanded with joy as she realized there was a healing taking place in both the children.

First thing in the morning the social worker was to arrive to look around. Abby had spent most of the evening making sure everything was neat and clean, looking at each room with an objective eye.

Although there was work that needed to be done in several areas of the house, she didn't think the social worker would count any of that against them. The house was clean, but had a lived-in feeling. It was obviously a home filled with warmth and love.

Making love to Luke again had deepened her feelings for him, and she knew eventually she'd be left with a heartache. She suspected that Luke's confession of being a recovering alcoholic had been an effort to warn her away. Just as he'd distanced her the first time they'd made love, she had a feeling he'd attempted to do the same the second time they'd made love.

But she knew in her heart, in her soul, that Luke was a good man, and she prayed that he would continue to stay strong and sober. Whether he was with her or not, she wanted that for him.

She sat straighter in the chair as she saw twin headlights pierce the night, heading in the direction of her house. Luke. Finally. She breathed a sigh of relief. She didn't realize how tense she'd been until some of that tension seeped out of her.

As the vehicle drew closer, her anxiety returned, exploding through her veins. It wasn't Luke's familiar pickup making its way toward the house, but an unfamiliar compact car.

Who was it? It was certainly too dark for her to be able to see the occupant of the car. Who would be driving to her house in the middle of the night?

Justin.

His name rang in her ears as fear turned her icy cold. Peaches, who'd fallen asleep on her lap, lifted her head and growled deep in her throat.

Abby put the dog on the floor and raced to the front door, assuring herself that it was locked tight. She grabbed the cordless phone and ran to the door, peering through the small diamond-shaped window in the wooden door.

The car pulled up directly in front of her porch and sat there idling for several long, torturous minutes. Knowing that Luke should be pulling in any minute, Abby was hesitant to call the sheriff, especially since at the moment she wasn't even positive it was Justin.

As she watched, the driver got out of the vehicle and stretched his arms overhead, as if he'd been driving a long distance and was stiff. As the moonlight fell full on his features, Abby recognized that it was, indeed, Justin.

Abby remained at the door and quickly punched in the numbers she had memorized that would ring the phone in the sheriff's office.

Sheriff Broder answered on the first ring.

"This is Abby Graham. Please come to my place quickly. I need help."

"On my way," Sheriff Broder responded.

As Abby punched the phone off, Justin sauntered to the front door. Heart pounding frantically, Abby put her weight against the door even though she knew in the back of her mind that no lock and certainly not her inconsequential body weight would keep Justin out if he wanted in.

"Abby." He knocked lightly on the door. Peaches growled, then barked low and deep in her puppy throat.

"Get out of here, Justin," she said, trying to keep her voice low enough so she wouldn't awaken Jason and Jessica. She didn't want them to experience the pulse-pounding fear that rocked through her.

"What's the matter, Abby? Do I make you nervous?" He chuckled, the sound once again turning Abby's blood to ice. He banged a fist against the door. Abby jumped and swallowed the scream that nearly escaped her.

"You bitch. You stole my kids. Did you think I wouldn't find you? Did you really think you could get away from me?'' He banged the door again, then laughed. ''Loretta always said I made her nervous.''

White-hot rage swept through Abby as he spoke her sister's name. He was the monster who had stolen Loretta from the people who loved her. ''I've called the sheriff, Justin. He'll be here any moment.''

Again he laughed, a wicked, evil sound that sent icy fingers up Abby's spine. ''Don't worry, Abby. When I decide to get you, you won't have time to call the sheriff. You won't have time to do anything.'' He didn't wait for her to reply, but walked off the porch and back to his car.

She watched as he drove off into the night, the darkness eventually swallowing the taillights of his car. She sagged against the door, hot tears scalding her cheeks.

They were tears of fear, tears of relief, and most of all, they were tears for the sister who was no longer with her. She was almost sorry Justin hadn't done something violent, something totally out of control that would see him permanently behind bars.

He'd only come for one thing, to mentally terrorize her. It had been a cat-and-mouse game. Damn him. Damn him to hell. And where…where was Luke?

She returned to her seat, Peaches once again in her lap, and stared out the window. At that moment she saw the whirling red lights that indicated Sheriff Broder was coming toward the house.

She met him on the porch and quickly explained to him what had happened. He seemed already to know that Luke was playing at the bar and assured Abby he would keep an eye on the place until Luke got home.

Abby went inside, assured by the presence of the sheriff but disturbed by Luke's absence. Where was he? Why wasn't he home yet? If he'd left as soon as he called, he should have been home by now.

As the seconds and minutes ticked by, her mind whirled with possibilities. Maybe he'd gotten held up at the party. One of the things she'd made clear to him was that she didn't expect him to change his lifestyle because of their marriage. But he said he'd be right home, a small voice niggled inside her head.

When an hour had passed, she fought the edges of panic that attempted to creep into her mind. She thought of calling one of Luke's relatives, but knew if nothing was wrong Luke would be angry at her decision.

And so she did nothing. She sat in the chair, staring into the darkness, a sentry guarding her children and waiting for the man she loved to return home.

She awakened with a start, torn from a horrible nightmare. She gasped and opened her eyes to brilliant morning sunshine pouring through the window and a wet tongue licking her cheek.

A new sense of panic ripped through her as she gazed at her watch and saw that it was seven-thirty and Luke still hadn't come home. The sheriff's car, which had been outside her home when she'd fallen asleep, was gone.

With a groan, she unfolded her stiff body and stood. The social worker would be here in an hour and a half, and somehow Abby had to act like everything was normal.

The first order of the day was to let Peaches outside.

When Peaches was finished with her business, Abby and the dog returned to the house. Abby checked on the children, who were still sleeping soundly, fed Peaches, then headed for a shower.

As she stood beneath the hot spray of water, her mind raced frantically. She thought of everything she had heard about Luke when he'd first come to work for her.

He drank too much, lived too fast, didn't take care of himself and took nothing seriously. He loved women and had a reputation as a charming rake. But she had come to see him as nothing like the man the rumors had portrayed.

She'd seen his innate warmth both with the children and with herself. She knew there was far more to the man than his reputation or the face he showed to the people in this town. Otherwise she wouldn't love him.

So, why hadn't he come home? And what should she do about it? She was nothing to him but a pleasant diversion. Theirs certainly wasn't a real marriage, it was a marriage created for the good of Jessica and Jason. What right did she have to set in motion a search? And how would such a search by the sheriff affect the custody suit?

But what if there had been an accident? What if Luke was hurt somewhere? What if he needed help? Oh, God, she was so confused.

By the time she got out of the shower, she'd made a decision. She would do nothing about Luke's absence until after the social worker left. She'd meet with Sonya Watkins and make a vague excuse about

Luke having to work. She'd pretend that everything was fine and pray that it would be.

But when Sonya Watkins left, Abby intended to tear up the phone lines, seeking Luke's whereabouts, no matter what the repercussions.

By the time she and the kids were dressed and had eaten breakfast and cleaned up the kitchen, Sonya Watkins had arrived.

Sonya was a plump woman in her mid-fifties who radiated confidence and warmth. She greeted Abby and the two children with a smile that was obviously meant to put them all at ease.

But Abby wasn't put at ease. She was aware that this woman with her cheerful smile and twinkling blue eyes was here to do a job and held an enormous amount of power as to the future of the children.

"What I would love to do first is see the children's bedrooms," she said. "Jason, would you like to show me your room?"

"Sure," Jason replied easily. He led the way down the hall to his room, Sonya following him and Jessica and Abby following Sonya.

Abby and Jessica stood in the doorway as Jason showed Sonya all the treasures his room contained. When Sonya had seen his book collection, his favorite truck, his ant farm and the rest of his goodies, she moved on to Jessica's room.

It was obvious she'd been told that Jessica didn't talk, for she asked no questions that would demand a reply from the little girl. She oohed and aahed over Jessica's stuffed animal collection and pretended to drink a cup of tea from a tiny plastic cup.

Abby returned to the kitchen and waited for Sonya to join her there. "Nice house," she said.

"Thank you. We still have some work to do, but my husband has already accomplished a lot."

"Yes, I expected to see your husband here this morning," Sonya said.

"Unfortunately, he got called away on business," Abby said, hoping the woman wouldn't pursue the subject. She didn't. She spoke to Abby about the children's routine, their school and their therapy.

Abby tried to stay cool and calm and answer all the questions, address any concerns, but her heart cried out. Where was Luke? Why wasn't he here? She prayed that wherever he was he was safe and unharmed.

Luke opened his eyes and instantly closed them to shut out the glare of the mid-morning sun. Dreaming. He had to be dreaming that he was in the alley behind the Honky Tonk.

He closed his eyes, for a moment drifted in a kind of foggy reality, then opened them once again.

It was still the alley. What was he doing here? What had happened? His mouth was dry, achingly dry. He started to sit up, then moaned and grabbed his head.

Hellfire, had he tied one on? He plucked at his shirt and wrinkled his nose. He certainly smelled like a brewery.

He'd never had a hangover like this. His skull felt as if it had been stuffed with rocks, and he felt disoriented, drugged.

Drugged.

Suddenly the fog fell away and he remembered. He'd had a restrained confrontation with Justin Cahill. Then he'd done something incredibly stupid—he'd downed a drink that had been sitting on the edge of the stage unattended.

Abby! Her name exploded in his head, and this time, ignoring the utter agony of his head, he jumped up from the ground and headed for his truck.

Let her be all right. Let Abby be all right. The words were a litany that raced around and around in his head as he pressed his foot firmly on the gas pedal.

Had Justin planned this? Had he drugged Luke to make certain he'd be out of the way, incapacitated? Had he left the Honky Tonk and driven to Abby's? Stormed the house and taken the children by force? Had Abby been hurt…or worse?

The fear that ripped through him was suddenly joined with a new emotion—rage. His rage was directed at the man who was at the bottom of all this.

Justin Cahill. If Luke discovered that he'd harmed Luke's wife or children, then Luke would personally hunt the man down and kill him with his bare hands.

As Luke turned into the driveway of the house, he was met by a car leaving. The driver of the car was a plump, gray-haired woman. She waved as they passed one another.

Relief made him gasp aloud as he saw Abby standing on the porch. He parked the truck, and before he got the door open, she was there.

He stepped out of the truck, and she threw herself into his arms. "Oh Luke, I've been worried sick," she said, her face buried in his chest. "I was so afraid something bad had happened to you."

"And I was so afraid that something had happened to you and the kids." He held her tightly for a moment, thanking the forces that had kept her safe through the long night.

She finally raised her head and gazed at him. "What happened, Luke? I was going to call the sheriff the minute the social worker left."

The social worker. In all the chaos, Luke had forgotten that Sonya Watkins was scheduled to do a home study that morning. He guessed she had been in the car that had passed him as he'd turned into the driveway.

"I'm sorry. How did it go with Mrs. Watkins?"

"I think it went okay, but what about you? Tell me what happened."

"Come on, let's go inside and I'll tell you what happened," he said. With his arm still around her shoulders, the two of them headed for the front door.

As they reached the door, she turned to him again, her nose wrinkled. "You stink," she exclaimed.

"Trust me, there's definitely more booze on me than there is in me. In fact, before I do anything, I want to take a shower."

"And while you shower, I'll make a pot of strong, hot coffee," Abby replied.

They parted in the living room, Luke heading for the bathroom and Abby for the kitchen. As Luke went into the bathroom he heard the sound of Jason and Jessica's laughter and Peaches' excited barking. No sound had ever sounded so good to his ears.

In the bathroom he stripped off his stinking clothes and jumped beneath the hot spray of water. What was Justin up to? Initially, Luke had thought the man had drugged him in order to gain access to Abby and the children. But Abby and the children appeared to be fine. So, what had been the point of drugging Luke? What had been the point of pouring alcohol all over him?

Almost as soon as the question zipped through his mind, the most logical answer followed. Luke knew the town of Inferno well enough to know that if one person had seen him in that alley, then most everyone in town would know he'd tied on a drunk and slept it off through the night.

He also knew that nobody in town would doubt the story. After all, a leopard didn't change its spots, and Luke had been known to drink too much before. But never before had it bothered him…what the town thought of him.

And now, Justin would be able to use where Luke had spent the night last night in the custody trial. All he'd have to do was call anyone in town who'd known that Luke had passed out.

That would certainly make an impression on a judge. And how devious and smart Justin had been to even think of such a thing. And how stupid Luke had been to be caught so off guard.

When he was dressed in clean clothes, he went into the kitchen where Abby had a mug of hot coffee waiting for him.

How on earth was he going to convince Abby he hadn't gotten stinking drunk and passed out? Given his reputation and the fact that he'd confessed to her that he was a recovering alcoholic, how was he going to convince anyone what really happened?

"You want to know where I've been all night?" he asked as he sat down next to her at the table. "I passed out and spent the night in the alley behind the Honky Tonk."

Her forehead wrinkled as she stared at him. "What do you mean, you passed out? I don't believe that for a minute," she said flatly.

He looked at her in surprise. "You don't believe me? Why not?"

"You aren't telling me everything," she said, her gaze holding his intently. "Something else happened. You didn't just get drunk and pass out."

"What makes you think that?"

She smiled and reached across the table to take his hand in hers. "Because I know you, Luke. Because you knew how important it was that you be here this morning for the home study...because you thought I might be in danger last night. And because I know you aren't the kind of man to blow off those things and just get drunk."

If he didn't believe her words, then he would have found it impossible to discount the light of belief that shone from her eyes. She believed him. She believed in him.

He pulled his hand from hers as emotion clogged his throat, making it impossible for him to speak. The idea that this woman who hadn't known him so very long, who'd heard all the rumors about his character yet believed in him filled him with a sense of awe he'd never before experienced.

He took a drink of his coffee, swallowed against the unfamiliar emotions, then explained to her what had happened. He told her about his meeting with Justin, the fact that Justin had had an opportunity to put something in his drink, and the moment he'd awakened remembering nothing after attempting to leave the Honky Tonk and get home to her.

"He came here. Last night Justin came here."

Luke sat up straighter in the chair. "What happened?" he asked as his blood began a familiar boil, the boil that had begun as he'd driven home.

"Nothing, really. I called Sheriff Broder, and he arrived just after Justin left." Although she looked perfectly calm and collected, there was a slight tremor to her voice that let him know she must have been terrified.

This time it was Luke who reached for her hand. Her hand felt small and vulnerable in his, and a wave of fierce protectiveness welled inside him.

"He didn't try to get in? He didn't try to hurt you?"

"No, nothing like that." She drew a deep breath. "He just frightened me," she confessed in a small voice.

Luke rose and pulled her into his arms, wanting…needing to shelter her, even though it was after the fact. She pressed against him in comfortable familiarity, and as always, her very nearness stirred Luke's senses.

Suddenly he was glad the custody suit would be resolved in ten days. The simple marriage agreement he'd entered into for the sake of the children all of a sudden didn't seem so simple anymore.

Chapter 14

"How about we go over to the ranch and take a trail ride?" Luke suggested the evening before the custody hearing. "The ranch went dark today, so we'll have the trails all to ourselves."

"Yeah, let's do that," Jason said with excitement. Jessica nodded eagerly.

"Even if I said no, it appears I would be outvoted," Abby said with a tired smile. "Go put on your jeans," she said to Jason and Jessica, who flew out of the room almost before the words were out of her mouth.

"Would you rather not go?" Luke asked.

"No, it sounds like fun. Anything to keep my mind occupied is welcome."

Luke fought the impulse to go to her, to pull her into his arms and assure her that everything would be all right. He hated seeing the tiny stress lines across her forehead, the lackluster of her eyes that indicated too little sleep.

Things had been tense since the night Justin had come here and Luke had been drugged. They had contacted Johnna and told her what had happened. Luke wasn't sure his sister had believed him, but she'd believed Abby that Justin had come to the house.

Johnna had filed for a restraining order against Justin, and since that day none of them had seen the dark-haired man whose appearance in Inferno had so dramatically changed their lives.

Within minutes the children were in the living room and ready to leave. They got into Abby's car and headed for the Delaney Dude Ranch.

Abby was quiet on the drive. She'd grown increasingly quiet and distant over the past week, and it was a distance Luke didn't know how to breach.

If he'd been a real husband, he would have held her through the darkness of the nights, forced her to talk about the fear and anxiety he knew filled her up. He would have shouldered as much of her burden as he could…if he'd been a real husband.

He'd already decided that if by some cruel trick of fate she lost the children tomorrow, he'd stick around her place for a couple of days to see that she was going to be okay. If she got custody, he'd pack up his things and move out tomorrow afternoon. Then in six months he'd leave Inferno and head to Nashville.

He waited for the burst of adrenaline he always felt when he thought of his future, but it was slow in coming. He chalked up his lack of enthusiasm to too much on his mind.

Tension had ripped through him, as well, for the past couple of days. He didn't trust Justin Cahill, kept waiting for the man to do something evil or underhanded.

Just as Luke had suspected, it hadn't taken long for the news of Luke's fall off the wagon to make the rounds of gossip.

Still, Johnna was optimistic about the hearing the next day, but Luke was worried what Justin might do if he lost. When he'd looked into Justin's eyes that night at the Honky Tonk, he'd sensed a man who would do anything...anything to get what he desired. And he wanted the children. Not because he loved them. Not because he wanted to make their lives better. But because he wanted the two million bucks that parental rights would put in his hands.

Even if Abby won custody, Luke decided he'd better hang out at the house for a couple more days to make certain that everything was all right.

He pulled into the ranch and parked near the stables. As the kids tumbled from the back seat, Luke reached across and grabbed Abby's arm to halt her exit from the car.

"Abby, we've done everything we can. There is absolutely nothing more we can do but try to enjoy today, all of us together."

Those green eyes of hers gazed at him, and in their depths he thought he saw an emotion that shouldn't be there. He thought he saw love.

He turned from her and exited the car, disturbed by what he thought he'd seen. Love had never been a part of this bargain. Love was the last thing that was supposed to happen.

As Abby climbed out of the car and the kids danced with excitement, Luke dismissed the craziness he thought he'd seen. He had to be mistaken. Abby was grateful to him. She loved what he had done for her. But she certainly didn't love him. Hell, even his own father, his own siblings had never really loved him.

Matthew, who was in the process of saddling up his horse, Thunder, met them outside the stables. He greeted them with his usual curt restraint.

"I thought I'd take Abby and the kids for a little trail ride," Luke explained.

"I'm getting ready to ride the fence lines and see what work needs to be done in the next month while we're dark," Matthew replied. He climbed on the back of the tall, spirited horse. "I understand tomorrow is an important day for you and your family. Good luck." With these words, he rode off.

Luke stared after his brother, wondering if any of them would ever be able to feel close to Matthew. Matthew seemed to be so tightly wound, so isolated.

It took thirty minutes for Luke to get everyone's horses saddled and ready to go. They'd ridden once before, earlier in the week, so the kids had overcome their fear of that first ride and were eager to get started.

It had been another perfect day, and the warmth of the sun had lingered into the evening hours, but it was not uncomfortably warm. There was just enough of a breeze to stir the air, kicking up the scents of earth and flowers and clean air.

They rode with Luke in the lead, then Jason, then

Jessica, then Abby bringing up the rear. When they hit open pasture, the kids rode side by side, and Luke fell back to join Abby.

She shot him a warm smile. "Thank you. This is just what I needed. The warmth of the sun, the sound of the kids laughing and a good and steady horse beneath me."

He returned her smile, feeling some of the tension that had gripped him in the past week easing. "I think we all needed this," he said. "It's been a long couple of weeks."

"And in some ways it's been the best couple of weeks in my whole life," she said.

He looked at her in surprise. "Why?"

She raised a hand from the reins and threaded it through her hair, and her beauty ached inside Luke's chest. "Three times in the last week I heard Jessica speak out loud to Peaches. Jason hasn't had a single nightmare in the last two weeks."

She frowned thoughtfully and returned her hand to the reins. "I don't really know quite how to explain it, but everything has seemed sweeter, more intense these last weeks." She sighed. "Maybe it's because I know there's a possibility that I'll lose everything tomorrow." She flashed him a bright smile. "But I'm not going to think about that today."

They rode for a few minutes in silence. It was a pleasant silence, broken only by Jason's chattering and an occasional burst of giggles from Jessica.

Tails switching, the horses plodded along the familiar trails at a sedate walk. The horses used for the guests were sweet-tempered and rarely spirited.

When they had been riding for about forty-five minutes, Luke insisted they stop and take a break. He knew that people who were unaccustomed to riding found muscles they didn't know they had after a brief time on the back of a horse.

They stopped at the same place where they had enjoyed their picnic the week before. The two children instantly began a game of tag while Abby and Luke sat in the shaded area beneath the trees. Luke allowed the horses to roam free, knowing they wouldn't go far and would return to him when he whistled.

As he stretched out his legs, Luke watched Abby watching Jason and Jessica as they played. The expression of joy that lit her face, the love she so obviously felt for the two, made her appear even more beautiful.

Luke knew he wouldn't make love to her again, that it wouldn't be right at this point in time. She was consumed with the custody fight, frightened about the future, and he had no intentions of being a part of that future.

He had two beautiful memories of the two of them making love together, memories that stirred him to distraction whenever he thought of those moments of passion. And he had a feeling making love to her one more time would only make their parting more difficult.

For the first time, he wondered what her life would be like after he was gone. "So, what are your plans once the custody issue is behind you?" he asked.

She pulled her knees to her chest and wrapped her

arms around them. "It depends on what the outcome is of the custody fight."

He smiled. "I'll rephrase the question. After you win custody of the kids tomorrow, what are your plans?"

She returned his smile, then frowned thoughtfully. "To be honest, I haven't given it a lot of thought. I've been so focused on tomorrow."

"Are you going to stay here in Inferno? Now that you can access your funds, you could live anywhere you want."

"We'll stay here," she said immediately. Her gaze shot to the two children playing tag. "Jason and Jessica love it here, and I must confess, I've fallen in love with Inferno."

She stretched her legs out before her. "I'll probably spend the next year while Jessica is in kindergarten not working. I'll get the rest of the house in order, then when she's in school full-time, I'll see about taking a teaching position."

"Sounds like a good life," he said softly.

"We're going to have a wonderful life." She said the words fervently, ferociously, as if she was less concerned in him believing them as believing them herself.

"I know you will," he replied, fighting a tiny bit of sorrow that he wouldn't be here to share it with her.

He stood and reached a hand out to pull her up. "We'd better get started back. The sun has started to go down."

She nodded and put her hand in his. He pulled her up, and for just a moment their bodies came together,

her breasts against his chest, her thighs against his. An instantaneous burst of heat swept through him, and he wondered if he'd ever again find a woman who stirred him on such a primal level.

She stepped quickly away from him, as if she'd felt the same flame of heat he had. Once again he thought he saw something flicker in the depths of her eyes, something tender, something that unsettled him.

"Jason, Jessica, come on, we're heading back," he called to the kids who were playing hide-and-seek nearby. It took ten minutes to get the kids settled on their horses and ready to head to the stables.

They had only ridden a short distance from the grove of trees when the sound of a gunshot split the air. Jessica and Jason screamed as adrenaline exploded inside Luke.

"Get off the horses! Get down on the ground," he yelled as another shot cracked resoundingly.

He slid off his horse and pulled the two kids down, keeping the horses between them and the area where he thought the shots had come from.

"Abby...Abby, get down," he commanded. She appeared to be in a daze, as if he wasn't making sense. Still holding the horses, with the terrified kids clinging to him, he grabbed Abby's arm to pull her down.

She slid off the horse and to the ground, and it was then Luke saw the red stain spreading out to take over the white of her T-shirt.

"Abby!" he cried in horror as she slumped to the ground.

"Mommy! Mommy!" Jason wailed, and Jessica screamed as Luke tried to calm the kids and assess

Abby's wound, all the while trying to keep behind the shelter of the horses.

"I'm all right," Abby said. "It's just my arm."

"Are you sure you're okay?" Luke asked urgently.

She nodded, her lower lip caught in her teeth.

"Stay here behind the horses. I'll be right back."

"No, Luke. Wait," she exclaimed as the children huddled by her side.

But he didn't listen to her. He left the cover of the horses and raced for the nearest grove of trees, a deadly rage rising inside him. Somebody had attacked his family. Somebody had shot his wife, and Luke knew who that somebody was. He wasn't about to let Justin Cahill get away.

He knew the general area where the shots had come from, and he raced swiftly, as silently as possible through the woods. He'd only run a few seconds before he heard the noise of somebody crashing through the underbrush, racing through the trees.

Cahill. The name pounded in his head and stoked the fires of anger to a fever pitch. He stopped long enough to listen, then followed the noise of running footsteps.

A figure ahead of him spurred him faster, and with a roar of rage, he hit Cahill in the back, tumbling both men to the ground. As Justin smashed down, the shotgun he'd been carrying flew out of reach.

Justin rolled to his back, and Luke jumped on top of him. "You son of a bitch. I'll kill you," Luke thundered as he smashed a fist into Justin's jaw.

Justin bucked and kicked in an attempt to escape,

but Luke straddled his prone body and delivered another blow, and another, and another.

"Luke...Luke, stop, you're going to kill him." Matthew's voice pierced the red haze that had descended in Luke's head.

Matthew grabbed Luke's arm as he reared back to deliver another hit. Luke stared up at his elder brother, his vision blurred by tears. "He attacked my family. Matthew...he shot Abby."

"I know, and you need to get Abby medical help. Go on. I'll take care of this scumbag," Matthew said, and for the first time Luke noticed he had a revolver in his hand.

Luke stood and Justin sat up, his eyes burning with hatred. "I hope I killed the bitch," he said. "She talked my wife into leaving me. She ruined my life."

Luke would have smashed the man's face again if Matthew hadn't cocked his gun. "Keep your mouth shut, you piece of dirt, and I'll try my best not to accidentally shoot you," Matthew said. "Go, Luke. Your family needs you."

His family needed him. Yes.

Abby. As he raced to where he'd left Abby and the children, his heartbeat frantic, the thudding rhythm of rage being replaced with the anxious beat of fear.

When he reached them, his fear grew overwhelming. A white pall had stolen the color from Abby's face, and her eyes were dull.

"Luke," she said weakly.

"It's all right. Everything is going to be just fine." He didn't take the time to explain. "We need to get you to the hospital." He tried not to focus on the blood that had completely soaked the white sleeve of her T-shirt.

"Jason…Jessica… I need you to stop crying and listen to me. I'm going to put you both on Abby's horse. Jason, you hold tight to the saddle horn, and Jessica, you hold tight to your brother, okay?"

Still sniffling, they nodded. He put the kids on the back of the horse, then went to Abby. "Abby…Abby, honey, we've got to get you out of here. I'm going to have to lift you up and put you on my horse. Can you lift your arms around my neck?"

She nodded, a faint movement of her head, then with a deep, wrenching moan, she lifted her arms and weakly clung to him.

It took him three attempts to mount the horse with her in his arms, but he finally managed to get up and hold her tight against his chest.

He grabbed the reins of the children's horse, and they took off, moving as fast as possible, the blood pounding in Luke's head as it seeped from Abby's body.

He was terrified that the jostling motion of the horse would make her wound worse, but the alternative was for her to bleed to death.

"Hang on, Abby…hang on," he said over and over again. But she didn't hang on. By the time they reached the car, she'd passed out.

Thirty minutes later Luke sat in the hospital waiting room, Jessica on his lap and Jason seated in the plastic chair next to his. They were waiting for the doctor to come out and tell them Abby's condition.

Luke barely remembered the drive to the hospital.

He'd never been so terrified in his life. She'd looked dead when he'd carried her into the emergency room, both he and the children screaming for help.

He held Jessica closer, realizing the little girl's hair smelled like Abby's. Abby's children. What would happen to them if Abby... He couldn't think about it. He couldn't imagine anything more horrible.

"Luke."

He looked up, surprised to see Sheriff Broder approaching him. "Heard you had some excitement out at the dude ranch," he said.

Gently Luke stood and put Jessica in his chair, then took Broder's arm and led him away from where the children were seated.

"Your brother came to see me about twenty minutes ago. He had a little surprise for me."

Luke nodded. "Cahill."

"Yup." A whisper of a grin lifted the corner of the sheriff's mouth. "Matthew had him trussed up like a calf. Told me that Cahill took a couple of shots at you and your family." Broder gestured toward the children. "I see the kids are okay."

"My wife. He shot my wife." Luke had never felt such bleak despair as when those words left his lips.

"Is she going to be all right?" Broder placed a hand on Luke's shoulder as if to steady him.

"I...I don't know. We're waiting to hear from the doctor."

"I need to get a report from you," Broder said, but at that moment Dr. Johnny Howerton entered the waiting room and strode toward Luke.

"We'll have to do this later," Luke said, his heart

banging in his chest as he anticipated what the doctor might say. "How is she?"

"She's weak and she was in shock, but she's stabilized. The shot was clean and took a dozen stitches, but she's conscious and she wants to see you."

"I'll stay here with the children," Sheriff Broder said.

Luke walked to Jessica and Jason. "This is the sheriff. He's going to wait here with you while I go in and see Mom for a minute."

"But I want to see her," Jason said, his little face streaked with dirt and tear tracks.

"I know, buddy. But for now she is in a place where only grown-ups can go in. I'll tell her you and Jessica love her and to get well real soon, okay?"

"Is she going to be all right?" Luke asked a moment later as he followed Dr. Howerton down the hallway.

"She was incredibly lucky. An inch one way or the other and that bullet would have done tremendous damage. As it is, she's going to have a sore shoulder for a while. I'd like to keep her a day or two for observation." He stopped outside the door to a semi-darkened room. "Just a few minutes, okay?"

Luke nodded and entered the room. Her eyes were closed and her face was as pale as the sheet that covered her. He wanted to see her eyes sparkling with life. He wanted to hear her laughter ringing in the air.

Luke sat in the chair next to the bed and gently took her hand in his.

"Abby? It's me, honey. It's Luke."

Her eyes fluttered open, and to his immense relief

her fingers tightened slightly around his. "Luke. I have to…I need to…"

"Sh," he whispered softly. "You're going to be all right. You've lost a lot of blood, but you're going to be fine."

"I have to go home," she said, a grimace twisting her features as she tried to sit up.

"You aren't going anywhere," Luke protested and gently pushed her against the pillows. "The doctor wants to keep you overnight."

"Overnight?" Her face was even paler than before, and a frown etched its way across her forehead.

"What?" he asked,

"The custody hearing…it's first thing in the morning. You have to go. You have to be there for me. Dress the kids nice…make sure their hair is combed…"

"I will. I promise," he said. He squeezed her hand once again. "You just rest and don't worry about a thing. Everything is going to be just fine."

"Justin? It was Justin, wasn't it?"

Luke nodded. "He's in jail now, and there's no way in hell he's going to get custody of those kids tomorrow. The son of a bitch took a gamble and he lost, Abby."

She closed her eyes, the grimace of pain momentarily easing. When she opened her eyes and looked at him again, her gorgeous green eyes were awash with tears.

"It's going to be all right, Abby," Luke said, his chest tight with emotion. He leaned forward and stroked a strand of her hair. "You want me to sit here with you for a while?"

"No, I want you to take the children home, feed them supper and tuck them into bed. I know they must be terrified and I want things as normal as possible for them. Please, Luke...promise me you'll take them home right now."

"I promise," he said, unable to deny her anything at the moment.

She closed her eyes, and her fingers went lax around his. He waited a moment or two, to see if she would speak or open her eyes again. She didn't, and finally he stood, leaned over and kissed her cheek, then left the room.

After telling Dr. Howerton to call him if any problems arose, he left the hospital and took his kids home.

They ate hot dogs and beans for supper, and while they ate, Luke explained to Jason and Jessica that Abby was fine, but the doctor wanted to keep her for a couple of days.

When they'd finished eating, Luke told the kids to get ready for bed and he would tuck them in. He let Peaches out to run, then let the dog back in and went into Jason's room.

"You all tucked in, buddy?" he asked as he sat on the side of the bed.

Jason nodded. "Can we go see Mom tomorrow?"

"You know we've got to go see the judge tomorrow morning, but after we're finished there, we'll go see your mom." Luke ruffled the little boy's hair, kissed him on the forehead, then moved to Jessica's room.

Jessica's big brown eyes pierced Luke's heart. He

saw in their depths fear, and although he repeated that her mommy was going to be fine and would be home in a couple of days and that in the meantime he'd keep her and her brother safe, he wasn't sure the little girl believed him.

After tucking in the kids, Luke went into the living room, where Peaches curled up next to him on the sofa.

Over and over again he replayed that moment when Abby had slumped from her horse to the ground, her T-shirt seeping blood. And over and over again he was filled with a sense of horror.

He never again wanted to see her so lifeless, so still. Never again did he want to see pain etching lines into her forehead, stealing away the sparkle of her eyes.

And never had he wanted a drink more than he did at this moment. He knew Abby had a bottle of wine in one of the cabinets in the kitchen. Although wine certainly wasn't his drink of choice, he knew a couple of glasses would take the edge off, relieve some of the tension that racked his body, erase some of the fear he felt each time he thought of Abby lying so pale, so lifeless.

He got up from the sofa and went into the kitchen, Peaches at his heels. He sat at the table and stared at the cabinet where he knew the wine was stored.

The kids were taken care of and sound asleep in their beds. Abby wasn't home. Nobody would know if he fell off the wagon.

Just one drink. It would make him feel better, dull all the emotions that thundered inside him. A vision of his father filled his head, a mental picture of the old man pacing the floor, bourbon splashing from the glass in one hand, a belt ready to strike in the other.

The beatings had always been worse when the old man had been drinking. Luke leaned back in the chair and dragged his hands down the sides of his face. Just one little drink. Nobody would know.

Except him. Until he took that drink, he was in charge of his life, his destiny. As Abby had told him, until he took that drink, he was a success.

Abby. He remembered her unshakable belief in him when he'd stumbled home one morning, reeking of alcohol Justin must have poured over him after he'd passed out in the alley. She hadn't questioned his story, had believed in him like no other person ever had in his life.

Suddenly the thirst he'd entertained was gone, vanished beneath the need to be the best he could be, not only for Abby, not only for the children, but also for himself.

"Come on, Peaches, it's time to go to bed. We have a big day tomorrow." He put Peaches in her bed, then, instead of stretching out on the sofa, went into Abby's bedroom. He wanted to sleep in Abby's bed with her sweet scent surrounding him.

As he walked into her bedroom, he spied the guitar he'd strung leaning against the wall next to her bed. He pulled down the sunflower bedspread, pulled off his T-shirt, then got in beneath the sheet.

He kept his jeans on, fearing that Jason might very well have one of his nightmares tonight. As he'd expected, the sheets smelled of Abby, and the room seemed filled with her spirit.

Closing his eyes, he tried to find sleep, knowing he'd need to be alert and clearheaded in the morning to face the family court judge. But sleep remained elusive. He was still too keyed up, too wired by the evening's events.

Abby white-faced, falling to the ground. Abby worried about her children despite her wounds. Abby... Abby...Abby.

He turned on the bedside lamp and grabbed the guitar. Strumming the strings in soft tones, he felt himself start to relax. He'd nearly finished the first tune when Jason appeared in his doorway.

"What's up, buddy?" he asked softly.

Jason shrugged his little shoulders. "I can't sleep." He rubbed his eyes. "Could I sleep in here with you, Luke?"

Luke patted the mattress next to him, and Jason eagerly jumped into the bed. Within minutes Jessica had joined them, cuddling up on the opposite side of Luke.

"Sing us a lullaby," Jason said. "Our mommy in Heaven used to sing us lullabies...before our daddy hurt her."

Luke's heart skipped a beat. Abby had told him the kids had never talked about that night, the night they had seen their father kill their mother.

"You saw your daddy hurt your mommy?" he asked lightly, still strumming the strings of the guitar.

"Mommy and Daddy were fighting, and she told us to go to our room, but we didn't," Jason said.

"Mommy was crying and Daddy hit her until she wasn't crying anymore," Jessica said.

"Remember that your mom and I talked about going to talk to the judge tomorrow?'' Luke asked. He continued to strum the guitar in soft, soothing tones. They both nodded. ''You think you could tell the judge what you saw your daddy do to your first mommy that night?''

They both frowned, obviously disturbed by the idea.

''It would really help your mommy now if you could do that,'' Luke continued. ''And the judge would make sure you never, ever had to see your daddy again.''

''And we could live together here forever?'' Jason asked.

''You and Jessica and your mommy and Peaches could live together forever, and you'd never have to be afraid again,'' Luke said.

Jason frowned for another long moment, then he shook his head. ''Then I'll tell the judge tomorrow.''

''Me, too,'' Jessica said softly.

''Now will you sing us a lullaby?'' Jason asked.

As Luke began to sing, Jessica and Jason snuggled against his sides. The scent of childhood clung to them, and he was awed by the fact that they had trusted him enough to tell him about the night of their mother's death.

Somewhere in the back of his mind, Luke wondered if Nashville could possibly be better than this.

Chapter 15

Abby awoke that morning knowing nothing on earth was going to keep her away from that custody hearing. In spite of the doctor's protests, despite an overwhelming lethargy and muscle aches that ripped through her, she left the hospital wearing a hospital gown tucked into her jeans and took a taxi to the courthouse where the hearing was going to take place.

She was early so she sat on a bench outside the courthouse, waiting for her family to arrive. Her family. Please God, let them continue to be her family.

She remembered Luke telling her that Justin was in jail for shooting her, but she was afraid he might somehow wiggle out of that, that even if they settled the custody issue today it would only be a temporary settlement and eventually she'd have to face Justin again…and again and again.

The sun was warm on her face, and the heat penetrated the gown where her shoulder was bandaged. It felt good, like the warmth of Luke's hands when they made love…like the warmth of his smile when he gazed at her.

Luke. Her time with him had been magical, and she wished the magic could go on forever. But he had big dreams, big hopes for finding magic in Nashville, and his future didn't include her.

After the hearing, it was time for her to set him free. He'd never intended the marriage to be permanent, and she'd promised him no strings, no regrets.

She would never let him know how much she would miss him, how much it would ache inside her when they said goodbye. She would never let him know how much she loved him…that she had a feeling she would always love him.

"Mommy!"

The cry called her from a half-sleep, and she opened her eyes to see Jessica and Jason racing toward her, Luke, handsome as a devil in a suit, following just behind them.

"Easy," she said to the kids as they raced into her arms. She hugged and kissed them, then stood and faced Luke.

"What on earth are people going to say? My wife sleeping on a bench in a hospital gown?" His eyes were teasing as he drew her against him. She welcomed his support, leaning against him for strength.

"I've never cared much what people say," she replied.

"I can't believe you're here. Did the doctor say it was okay?" he asked worriedly.

She smiled sheepishly. "Let's just say he was not particularly enthusiastic about letting me go. But I couldn't miss this. I had to be here."

At that moment Johnna arrived, gray eyes twinkling as she eyed the group. "This is going to be a cakewalk," she said merrily. "I can't believe that man was so stupid as to get himself arrested the night before this hearing."

"I just wish it was on a charge that would put him away forever," Abby said softly.

Luke held her closer, and Abby fought a sudden burn of tears. She'd once believed she couldn't live without her children, and now she had to figure out how she was going to live without the man she loved.

"Come on, let's go get this done," Johnna said. "I have a feeling the judge won't look kindly on a man who would discharge a firearm in the direction of his children. I believe what he did to you is considered attempted murder, and there's no way he isn't going to face that charge."

Abby nodded, somehow not assured by Johnna's words. He'd gotten away with murder before...why not attempted murder?

Together the five of them entered the courthouse.

Abby wasn't sure what she'd expected, but the hearing was surprisingly short and rather informal. The judge, an elderly man with a snowy head of hair and piercing blue eyes, indicated that he had a favorable home study report from Sonya Watkins.

Shock riveted through Abby when Sheriff Broder arrived with Justin in tow. The children became obviously upset, and the judge took them back with him to his chambers.

As they waited for the judge to return, Luke's hand grabbed hers, and in a whispered tone he told her what had happened with the children the night before, how they had indicated that they would tell the judge what had happened the night their mother was killed.

Abby said nothing, but her heart filled with an amazing joy and an intense pain. Luke had proven to Jessica and Jason that he was a good man, and they had trusted him with their secrets.

They would miss him when he was gone, this man who had sung them lullabies. And her heart would break when it came time for her to say goodbye to him.

She glanced at Justin, who cast her a cocky smile. The man had tried to kill her. Without a doubt she knew that had been his intention. He'd wanted her out of the children's lives, permanently out of the way. And she saw in his eyes a promise…the promise that this wasn't over.

A wave of hopelessness shot through her. How much time would he get for shooting her? Enough time so that when he got out of jail the children would be grown? Somehow she didn't think so. She had long ago lost faith in the judicial system and knew it was possible Justin would get off with a slap on the wrist and probation.

Luke wrapped his fingers around hers, as if sensing her anguished thoughts. Again she wondered what she was going to do without him. Since their marriage, for all intents and purposes they had interacted like a real family. And more than anything, Abby wished they could continue to be a family forever.

As the minutes clicked by, Abby wondered what was going on between the judge and the children. What if despite what they'd told Luke the night before, they simply couldn't bring themselves to talk to the judge?

Finally the judge returned to the bench, his features sternly forbidding. ''I have just spoken to the children at length. I find them to be bright and articulate, and you are to be commended, Mr. and Mrs. Delaney, for their adjustment to life after their mother's death.''

''Your Honor, I appreciate everything that Abby has done for my children in my absence from their lives, but I am their father and I have a right to have my children back with me,'' Justin said.

''Mr. Cahill, even if I were to discount the circumstances involving the shooting last night, even if I were to believe your story that the shooting was accidental and you had no intention of harming anyone, I cannot discount what the children told me concerning the night of your wife's murder.''

Justin looked stricken, and Abby knew he had been confident the children would remain too traumatized to ever discuss that night with anyone.

''I have been in touch with the district attorney in Kansas City, Missouri,'' the judge continued. ''And in light of this new information, they inform me that they intend to go to trial once again and charge you with first-degree murder. Therefore, in the best interest of the children, I terminate your parental rights and grant permanent custody to Luke and Abby Delaney." The judge banged his gavel. "Court dismissed."

Justin erupted with shouted curses and threats. Luke grabbed Abby and hugged her, and Johnna did the same. Abby clung to them both, unable to believe that it was over.

Broder led a still screaming Justin from the courtroom, and the judge released the children from his chambers. Again there were hugs all around as Abby told them they were going to live with her forever.

"I'd love to continue a long celebration," Luke said. "But we need to get this woman back to the hospital."

"No...please. I just want to go home," Abby said. "I'll call the doctor from there and get all his instructions. Please, Luke. Let's all go home."

Now that the drama of the moment was over, Abby was beyond weary, and her shoulder ached with an unrelenting, throbbing pain.

But they had won! Tears of joy spilled down her cheeks as she realized the children would never have to spend a day...a minute with their father. She and the children could build a good life together without looking over their shoulders, without being afraid.

And if what the judge had said was true, Loretta's murder would finally be vindicated. Justin would be returned to Kansas City to stand trial again, and this time she knew the children would be strong enough to voice what had happened on that horrible night. It was over. Finally.

For the next four days, Abby spent most of her time in bed as Dr. Howerton had instructed. Luke insisted that he cook the meals, and it was one of the few things Abby realized he did not do well. Each evening at supper they all spent the first few minutes of the meal trying to guess what the ingredients were of whatever he had cooked.

And every night Abby lay in bed, dreading the day when Luke would leave, knowing the time was coming far too quickly for her. With each day that passed, she felt Luke subtly distancing himself from them all. Not in big ways, but in small ways that told her he was preparing both her and the children for his absence.

Exactly one week after the custody hearing, the day after they got the news that Justin had been extradited to Missouri to stand trial again, Luke began to pack what few belongings he'd brought to the house.

His truck was packed and ready to go just minutes before it was time for the children to get home from school. Abby wondered if he'd timed it that way on purpose. He would leave as the children arrived home, giving her no time to grieve his leaving.

"It's not like we'll never see each other again," Luke said as the two of them stood next to his truck. "It's still months before I leave town."

She nodded, her mind embracing the vision of him. Those strong, bold features of his would be forever emblazoned in her memories. Her fingertips would always retain the feel of his wide, muscular shoulders, the springy hair of his broad chest, the warmth of his skin.

Her heart would treasure forever the laughter they

had shared, the dramas and joys of their time together. Her soul would always cherish and remember her love for him.

For a long moment his gaze held hers. She didn't want him to go yet couldn't stop him. She'd promised and, just like he always kept his promises, she always tried to keep hers.

It was he who averted his gaze first, staring toward the road where a cloud of dust indicated the approach of the school bus. "You and the kids will be fine," he said, and it sounded like he was assuring himself more than her.

"Yes, we'll be fine," she agreed softly. And they would. Abby was strong, stronger than she'd ever believed herself to be, and she knew she would survive this even though her heart was breaking into tiny, shattered pieces.

"Johnna will send over the divorce papers. They should be cut and dried."

Again Abby nodded, unable to speak as emotion rose in her throat.

With a squeal of brakes, the big yellow bus lumbered to a halt, and Jason and Jessica got off. They raced toward Luke and Abby, their faces lit with happiness.

Jason's smile fell first as he saw Luke's things in the back of the truck. "Where are you going, Luke?"

Luke bent on one knee and drew Jason and Jessica close to him. "It's time for me to go back to my own house. I was just staying here with you guys while I worked on the place and while we were waiting for the judge to make a decision."

"Where's your house?" Jason asked.

"You know the ranch where we ride the horses? That's where I'm going to be living now."

Jessica's lower lip quivered slightly. "But Peaches is gonna miss you," she said softly and put a little hand on Luke's cheek. "You're our lullaby man. Who is gonna sing us lullabies?"

Luke stood, as if needing to distance himself from the children. "Your mommy can sing you lullabies," he said.

"No, she can't." Jason wrinkled his nose. "She doesn't sing good at all."

A burst of half-hysterical laughter left Abby's lips. "Now you know the last of my secrets. I'm pretty much tone-deaf." The laughter died on her lips, and she swallowed hard against a sob that threatened to erupt. "You two better go see your dog. She's been waiting for you all day long."

Jason and Jessica gave Luke one final look then headed for the house.

"Then I guess this is it," Luke said, his gaze once again not meeting hers.

"Yes."

"But we'll see each other around." His beautiful gray eyes looked at her for a long moment. "This is for the best, Abby. You don't need a man like me in your life."

"You mean I don't need a strong, wonderful, loving man?"

He didn't reply, but instead climbed into his truck, started the engine and took off.

Abby watched his truck pull away, the tears she had

tried so hard to contain once again burning...oozing uncontrollably down her cheeks.

Luke. Luke. Her heart cried out for him. Her soul mate. The children's lullaby man. Gone.

She turned, stumbled to the porch and sank down, half-blinded by the tears that continued to flow down her face. She'd known all along that this day would come, had believed she was prepared for it.

What she hadn't been prepared for was the utter, profound, intense heartache of loving Luke.

"Mom, can we have some cookies?" Jason asked as he flew out the front door.

"Sure," she replied, not turning to look at him. "You can each have two cookies and a glass of milk."

"You sound funny." Jason sat next to her and looked at her. "You're crying."

Abby hurriedly swiped at her cheeks. "Maybe just a little," she replied.

"Are you hurt?" He looked at her worriedly.

"No, I'm not hurt on the outside, but my heart hurts."

Jason's eyes narrowed. "Did Luke hurt your heart?"

"Maybe just a tiny little bit," she said, then swiped her eyes. "But Luke didn't mean to hurt my heart." She gave Jason a hug and forced a wide smile. "But don't you worry. I'll be fine. We're all going to be fine. Come on, let's go get some cookies and milk."

Luke had believed that in making the break, in packing up and leaving Abby, he'd feel relief. After all, it had never been intended to be a lasting marriage.

They had accomplished their goal, and now it was time for him to focus on his future.

But as he drove away from the house, he felt no relief, and he felt no real thrill of anticipation when he contemplated his future.

The lullaby man. He remembered the night Abby had been shot, when he and the children had been together in her bed and he'd sung every lullaby he could think of to the two worried children.

There had been a special peace inside him as he'd smelled the scent of childhood clinging to them, had watched their eyes grow heavy with sleep and had seen their smiles of pleasure as he'd sung them to slumberland.

Would he ever have a better audience? All he had ever wanted to accomplish in his life was to prove to his old man that he could be somebody important…be somebody special. And wasn't he that to Abby's children? He was their lullaby man.

He hadn't expected to hurt when he walked away from them, and yet pain radiated through his chest directly into his heart.

It was a familiar pain, the pain he'd felt as a child when he'd realized no matter what he did, his father wouldn't love him. It was the same ache he'd felt as a young man, displaced and alone despite his family. It was the gnawing agony that always in the past had made him reach for a drink.

He pulled his truck to the side of the road and shut off the engine, needing to think. Everything suddenly seemed all jumbled up in his head.

He hadn't expected to fall in love with Jason and

Jessica, and he told himself it was saying goodbye to them that had confused him, unsettled him. He hadn't realized until this moment just how deeply they had crept into his heart.

Abby loved him. He knew it as surely as he knew his own name. As he'd told her goodbye, in those moments when their gazes had locked, he'd seen her love…unabashed, unadorned and unhidden. It had flowed from those beautiful eyes of hers and momentarily filled up every dark space and every lonely place in his heart.

She loved him and she believed in him. He leaned his head back and closed his eyes, thinking of that morning when he'd come home stinking of booze. She had believed his story without reservation because she knew what kind of man he was and believed the best of him.

Now all he had to figure out was what kind of a man he was and what he really wanted for himself.

Abby and the two children had just finished their cookies and milk when a knock fell on the front door. "I'll get it," Jason exclaimed, flying from his chair and racing for the door with Peaches and Abby at his heels.

Jason pulled open the door, and Luke stepped in. "Hi, Jason," he said.

Without warning, Jason drew back his leg and kicked Luke hard in the shin.

"Jason!" Abby yelled as Luke yelped and Peaches barked.

"I told him," Jason said, his little chin raised defiantly. "I told him that if he ever hurt you I'd kick him really hard. He hurt you and made you cry."

"Go to your room, young man," Abby exclaimed, appalled by Jason's actions. As Jason stalked off down the hall, Luke hobbled to the sofa and sank down.

"Don't be too hard on him," Luke said as he rubbed his shin.

"I'm so sorry," Abby exclaimed, trying to figure out why he was back, trying to ignore how her heart leaped at the sight of him. "Did you forget something?" she asked.

He straightened up. "Yeah, I did. I forgot that I promised you I'd build you new kitchen cabinets. I never got them finished."

"That's not necessary now," she murmured. "Besides, it wasn't a real promise. It was just something you mentioned."

"No." He stood with a shake of his head. "I distinctly remember it was a promise, and I told you I never break my promises."

Abby felt as if she were involved in some sort of emotional warfare. Didn't he realize she didn't want him coming here everyday, working in her kitchen, indulging in flirtatious banter, then leaving each night to go back to his own life?

She didn't want him to build cabinets. She didn't want him to wash the windows or take out the trash. All she wanted was for him to love her. She held her tongue as Jessica came into the living room from the kitchen.

"Sweetie, why don't you go get your brother and

the two of you can play outside on the swing for a little while," she said.

Jessica nodded, and Luke and Abby said nothing until the kids had disappeared out the front door. "Luke, I don't think it's a good idea, you coming back and forth here to do any work."

She was pleased at how unemotional she'd managed to sound, pleased that her voice didn't betray the tumultuous emotions his mere presence had stirred in her.

"You're right. I don't think that's a good idea, either." He advanced toward her, his gaze holding hers. "I think it's best if I just stay here until all the work around this place is completed. And I figure with the hours I have to put in at the ranch and my woodworking business, the work around here should take about thirty or forty years to complete."

She frowned and looked at him in confusion. "What are you talking about?" she asked. This time her voice caught with emotion.

He stood mere inches from her, the familiar masculine scent of him surrounding her. "I'm talking about forever, Abby. I'm talking about making love to you every night and waking up with you in my arms every morning." He placed his hands on either side of her face. "I'm talking about watching Jason at his first Little League game and taking Jessica to her first dance recital."

Abby's heart had begun the rhythm of hope, of love, but she knew of Luke's dreams and would not, could not be the reason he didn't pursue them. "But...what about Nashville?"

Luke dropped his hands from her face and stepped back from her. He grabbed her hand and led her to the sofa where they both sat down.

"Nashville was the dream of a boy," he said. "A boy whose father had told him thousands of times how worthless he was. So that boy dreamed of being a star, of being rich and famous…somebody important to show his old man."

He smiled and tightened his fingers around her hand. "And then an amazing thing happened. He looked into the eyes of a beautiful woman and saw that he *was* somebody important. I love you, Abby. And when you look at me, I feel like I'm king of the world. And if I turn my back on our love, then I truly am the fool my father always told me I was."

"Oh, Luke." Tears sprang to Abby's eyes, and she started to reach for him but paused as he held up a hand to stop her.

"I want you to understand something, Abby. I'm an alcoholic, and I'll always have to fight that battle one day at a time."

"When I had Justin hanging over my head, that's how I learned to survive," she said softly. "One day at a time. I couldn't anticipate the future, nor could I dwell upon the past."

His eyes, those beautiful, long-lashed eyes gazed at her intently. "I realize now I drank to forget instead of working to heal the wounds left by my father. But you loving me…the kids trusting me, that's done more to heal me than I ever thought possible. I love you, Abigail Delaney."

Abby threw herself into his arms, unable to stand not being there for another minute. "I love you, Luke. I have never loved anyone as much as I love you. But I want you to be sure. You're giving up your dreams."

"Darlin', I've never been more certain of anything in my entire life." His smoky eyes gazed into hers with an intensity that threatened to steal her breath away. "And all I'm doing is trading dreams. I'm trading in the dreams of a child for the dreams of a man. You and the children, you're my real dream."

She leaned into him and touched her lips to his, needing to kiss him, wanting to show him just how very much he meant to her.

Their kiss was hungry, fevered with emotion, salted by Abby's tears of happiness. He was the man she'd dreamed of in the darkest, most lonely hours of the night. He was not a knight and not a knave, but simply the man she wanted to spend the rest of her life loving.

She'd hoped...she'd prayed that eventually she'd find a man strong enough to lean on, yet gentle enough to parent the two children who would require plenty of patience and understanding. And fate had delivered Luke to her doorstep...the answer to her prayers.

"I think I fell in love with you that very first day I met you," he said when their kiss finally ended.

"That was lust, not love," she said teasingly.

He grinned. "Trust me, I lust for you and probably will continue to lust for you until we're both old and gray. But I know the difference between lust and love. And I love you, Abby. I don't want a divorce. All I want is to be a good husband to you and a good father to Jason and Jessica." And with these words he claimed her lips again in a kiss of infinite love.

Tears of joy coursed down Abby's cheeks. He ended the kiss and smiled at her. "Please...please wipe those tears away. If Jason sees them, he's liable to cripple me for life."

Abby laughed through her tears, and with his fingertips he gently wiped the tears away. "Promise me..." she began, her love for him so intense it shimmered inside her like a million brilliant lights. "Promise me we'll weather the storms of life together. Promise me that you'll love me forever."

He grinned, that lazy, sexy grin that always lit a fire in the depth of her soul. "That's the easiest promise I've ever made." Again he placed his palms on the sides of her face. "I promise that I'm going to love you until the day I die, and even in death, we'll find each other and share eternity loving each other."

"And I promise the same thing," she replied, wondering if it were possible for her to be any happier than she was at this very moment.

"I'm not singing down at the Honky Tonk anymore," he said. "The only singing I want to do now is for Jessica and Jason. They are the best audience I could ever have."

"We need to go tell them that you're going to stay, that you're going to be their daddy from now until forever."

"Yeah, we need to tell them. But first..." He stood and pulled her into his arms for another kiss, this one filled with passion, with commitment, with love.

Abby's heart sang with the knowledge that this was only the beginning for them…the beginning of a life together and of dreams realized. They were now, truly and forever, a family.

* * * * *

THE DELANEY HEIRS
series will continue.
Watch for Matthew's story,
coming in May from
Silhouette Intimate Moments.

■ Silhouette®

INTIMATE MOMENTS™

presents

Romancing the Crown

*With the help of their powerful allies,
the royal family of Montebello is
determined to find their missing heir.
But the search for the beloved prince
is not without danger—or passion!*

Available in February 2002:
THE PRINCESS AND THE MERCENARY
by Marilyn Pappano

*This exciting twelve-book series begins in
January and continues throughout the year
with these fabulous titles:*

January	(IM #1124)	THE MAN WHO WOULD BE KING by Linda Turner
February	(IM #1130)	THE PRINCESS AND THE MERCENARY by Marilyn Pappano
March	(IM #1136)	THE DISENCHANTED DUKE by Marie Ferrarella
April	(IM #1142)	SECRET-AGENT SHEIK by Linda Winstead Jones
May	(IM #1148)	VIRGIN SEDUCTION by Kathleen Creighton
June	(IM #1154)	ROYAL SPY by Valerie Parv
July	(IM #1160)	HER LORD PROTECTOR by Eileen Wilks
August	(IM #1166)	SECRETS OF A PREGNANT PRINCESS by Carla Cassidy
September	(IM #1172)	A ROYAL MURDER by Lyn Stone
October	(IM #1178)	SARAH'S KNIGHT by Mary McBride
November	(IM #1184)	UNDER THE KING'S COMMAND by Ingrid Weaver
December	(IM #1190)	THE PRINCE'S WEDDING by Justine Davis

*Available only from Silhouette Intimate Moments
at your favorite retail outlet.*

 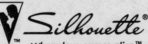

■ Silhouette®
Where love comes alive™

Visit Silhouette at www.eHarlequin.com   SIMRC2

CRIMES OF

Passion

Sometimes Cupid's aim can be deadly.

This Valentine's Day, Worldwide Mystery brings you
four stories of passionate betrayal and deadly crime
in one gripping anthology.

Crimes of Passion features FIRE AND ICE,
NIGHT FLAMES, ST. VALENTINE'S DIAMOND,
and THE LOVEBIRDS by favorite romance authors
Maggie Price and B.J. Daniels,
and top mystery authors Nancy Means Wright
and Jonathan Harrington.

Where red isn't just for roses.

Available January 2002 at your favorite retail outlet.

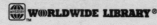

WORLDWIDE LIBRARY ®

WCOP

Silhouette —

where love comes alive—online...

eHARLEQUIN.com

your romantic magazine

━Romance 101━━━━━
♥ Guides to romance, dating and flirting.

━Dr. Romance ━━━━━
♥ Get romance advice and tips from
our expert, Dr. Romance.

━Recipes for Romance ━━
♥ How to plan romantic meals for you
and your sweetie.

━Daily Love Dose━━━━
♥ Tips on how to keep the romance
alive every day.

━Tales from the Heart━━
♥ Discuss romantic dilemmas with other
members in our Tales from the Heart
message board.

All this and more available at
www.eHarlequin.com

SINTL1R2

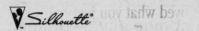

INTIMATE MOMENTS™

THE VALENTINE TWO-STEP,
IM #1133

**The first book in RaeAnne Thayne's new
Western miniseries**

♡UTLAW HARTES

*This time they're on the right side of the law—
and looking for love!*

*Available in February only from
Silhouette Intimate Moments.*

Be on the lookout for

**TAMING JESSE JAMES,
IM #1139 (March 2002)**

**CASSIDY HARTE AND THE COMEBACK KID,
IM #1144 (April 2002)**

Available at your favorite retail outlet.

Silhouette®
Where love comes alive™

Visit Silhouette at www.eHarlequin.com   SIMOH

If you enjoyed what you just read,
then we've got an offer you can't resist!

Take 2 bestselling love stories FREE!

Plus get a FREE surprise gift!

Clip this page and mail it to Silhouette Reader Service™

IN U.S.A.	**IN CANADA**
3010 Walden Ave.	P.O. Box 609
P.O. Box 1867	Fort Erie, Ontario
Buffalo, N.Y. 14240-1867	L2A 5X3

YES! Please send me 2 free Silhouette Intimate Moments® novels and my free surprise gift. After receiving them, if I don't wish to receive anymore, I can return the shipping statement marked cancel. If I don't cancel, I will receive 6 brand-new novels every month, before they're available in stores! In the U.S.A., bill me at the bargain price of $3.80 plus 25¢ shipping and handling per book and applicable sales tax, if any*. In Canada, bill me at the bargain price of $4.21 plus 25¢ shipping and handling per book and applicable taxes**. That's the complete price and a savings of at least 10% off the cover prices—what a great deal! I understand that accepting the 2 free books and gift places me under no obligation ever to buy any books. I can always return a shipment and cancel at any time. Even if I never buy another book from Silhouette, the 2 free books and gift are mine to keep forever.

245 SEN DFNU
345 SEN DFNV

Name	(PLEASE PRINT)	
Address	Apt.#	
City	State/Prov.	Zip/Postal Code

* Terms and prices subject to change without notice. Sales tax applicable in N.Y.
** Canadian residents will be charged applicable provincial taxes and GST.
 All orders subject to approval. Offer limited to one per household and not valid to current Silhouette Intimate Moments® subscribers.
 ® are registered trademarks of Harlequin Enterprises Limited.

INMOM01   ©1998 Harlequin Enterprises Limited

The unforgettable sequel to *Iron Lace*

RISING TIDES

Aurore Gerritsen left clear instructions: Her will is to be read over a four-day period at her summer cottage on a small Louisiana island. Those who don't stay will forfeit their inheritance. With a vast fortune at stake, no one will take that risk. Suspicions rise as Aurore's lawyer dispenses small bequests, each designed to expose the matriarch's well-kept secrets. Family loyalties are jeopardized and shocking new alliances are formed. But with a savage hurricane approaching, tensions reach a dangerous climax. And the very survival of Aurore's heirs is threatened.

EMILIE RICHARDS

"...a multi-layered plot, vivid descriptions, and a keen sense of time and place."
—*Library Journal*

Available the first week of January 2002 wherever paperbacks are sold!

MIRA®

Visit us at www.mirabooks.com

MER888

Silhouette

INTIMATE MOMENTS™
and *USA TODAY* BESTSELLING AUTHOR
RUTH LANGAN
present her new miniseries

Lives—and hearts—are on the line when the Lassiters pledge to uphold the law at any cost.

Available March 2002
BANNING'S WOMAN (IM #1135)

When a stalker threatens Congresswoman
Mary Brendan Lassiter, the only one who can help is a
police captain who's falling for the feisty Lassiter lady!

Available May 2002
HIS FATHER'S SON (IM #1147)

Lawyer Cameron Lassiter discovers there's more to life than fun
and games when he loses his heart to a beautiful social worker.

And if you missed them,
look for books one and two in the series

BY HONOR BOUND (IM #1111)
and
RETURN OF THE PRODIGAL SON (IM #1123)

Available at your favorite retail outlet.

Silhouette®
Where love comes alive™

Visit Silhouette at www.eHarlequin.com   SIMLL02

INTIMATE MOMENTS™

Where Texas society reigns supreme—and appearances are everything!

When a bomb rips through the historic Lone Star Country Club, a mystery begins in Mission Creek....

Available February 2002
ONCE A FATHER (IM #1132)
by Marie Ferrarella
A lonely firefighter and a warmhearted doctor fall in love while trying to help a five-year-old boy orphaned by the bombing.

Available March 2002
IN THE LINE OF FIRE (IM #1138)
by Beverly Bird
Can a lady cop on the bombing task force and a sexy ex-con stop fighting long enough to realize they're crazy about each other?

Available April 2002
MOMENT OF TRUTH (IM #1143)
by Maggie Price
A bomb tech returns home to Mission Creek and discovers that an old flame has been keeping a secret from him....

And be sure not to miss the Silhouette anthology

Lone Star Country Club: The Debutantes

Available in May 2002

Available at your favorite retail outlet.

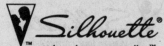

Where love comes alive™

Visit Silhouette at www.eHarlequin.com   SIMLCC